Family Tithes

By Colette Tozer

Editing & cover art by Rodney Tozer

ISBN: 978-0-9981534-3-8

First Published by Tozer Publishing 2016

www.TozerPublishing.com

Prologue

The mother was out.

The fire was crackling back at its admirer and the night was still, quiet and for everyone else on that same block; abundantly peaceful.

As for that particular household, however, the evil within was stirring; brooding and culminating.

The entirety of the household, save for the mother, who was as always, happy to be blissfully ignorant, knew that it was only a matter of time.

Eventually, the simmering fetor of disdain was bound to come to fruition.

Inevitably, the mask would be peeled away, revealing the true stench of rot and decay that congealed right beneath the surface.

However, for the moment, this house was as quiet as the rest of the neighborhood.

At present, the fire was the only source of light.

The admirer of the blazing, primal form of cleansing was the father.

One of his two boys sat on the floor of their sprawling, gothic-styled living room, in front of the fireplace that was so large, that a grown man could fit inside it.

The boy was playing with blocks and becoming quite bored with the amusement.

The father caught his son within his gaze.

Yet, instead of a sense of pride, like most fathers would feel in a moment like this, all Dr. Alexander Krone felt was disdain.

Although, the hint to his true feelings did not present itself on the father's face for long. For, with a comforting thought, his expression quickly changed to what appeared to be a friendlier disposition.

He beamed, now trying his best to appear utterly approachable.

"Eric, come here, boy. I have something for you."

The soft, welcoming voice was fairly out of character for his father when he was out of his mother's earshot and so, the boy glanced up at him inquisitively.

"Come on. Come here. I've got a present for you."

The boy stood up and looked around for his older brother, who he hadn't seen since his father had sat down in the large, crimson, carved mahogany, Lion Gothic Throne Chair that he had claimed solely as his own. The throne overlooked the lavishly garnished fireplace, positioned in a manner that allowed Dr. Krone to always have a keen vantage point to all of his surroundings.

He did this so that he would never be caught off guard. It always seemed that he managed to maintain a lead of at least two steps, not only in front of his sons but anyone else who might wish to do him harm.

Dr. Krone had a lot of enemies, but few worthy rivals.

Nonetheless, Krone was always prepared.

This knowledge ran through Eric's mind as he contemplated his next action. While he couldn't possibly, truly understand what his father was capable of, he did know that he shouldn't trust the man.

His eyes searched the old man's strange expression before tearing himself away to find a clue as to where his older brother had gone.

When he couldn't decipher where Derrick had gone, Eric's attention returned to his father.

Dr. Krone tried to be patient. Although his passivity had its strict limits, he was well aware of the situations where it would suit him to exercise his capacity for endurance.

Thus, he waited for the child's gaze to return to his.

His wide eyes stared distrustfully, yet curious.

After all, all children like presents and since he was usually shielded from many of the horrors inherent in his father's true nature, Eric still held out hope that his father could change.

For as intelligent as he was, even at the age of three, the child was still naive to the true evils of the world, despite the fact that he was spawned by and lived with a man who was inherently and particularly nefarious.

His older brother had a lot to do with the reasons behind Eric's weariness.

Even at his tender age, his brother had instilled a fear of his father that had nothing to do with paternal respect.

Therefore, the child had reservations, but not enough to make him run the other way.

"What is it?" Eric finally asked, stepping towards his father a few more paces.

Dr. Krone leered darkly but the boy mistook it for affability.

"It's a surprise. Come over here and I'll give it to you."

The boy knew that he shouldn't take anything from his father without first clearing it with his brother, but since his brother was nowhere to be found, Eric continued forward.

Although, when he was more than halfway across the space that divided them, he had second thoughts.

After all, it wasn't like his brother to be too far away when his father was home. He never trusted anything he did and it was strange that he would leave him alone with the man for the better part of an hour without at least checking in on him to ensure he was alright.

Eric wasn't quite sure why that was, but since his father was gone more often than he was at home, the boy trusted Derrick more than anyone.

"Where's Derrick?" The boy asked suspiciously.

"He's upstairs, watching television." His father answered as though he had prepared himself for the inquiry.

"I don't hear it."

"It's a large house." He snapped, but automatically softened his tone. "Besides, why do you care what he's doing? I have something for you, not him." Dr. Krone reached into the overcoat of his perfectly pressed, overcoat pocket and pulled out a large, imported chocolate bar. "I picked this up whilst amid my travels. It is truly an exotic treat." He sneered. "It's like nothing you've ever tasted before, I assure you."

"Chocolate?" Eric's eyes grew large as his father nodded.

The temptation was mounting, even though his brother's voice rang solidly in the back of his mind, warning him against taking anything edible from his father.

*He will hurt you...*Eric specifically remembered his brother telling him. *I don't mean to scare you, but I don't want to see anything happen to you. Promise me...*

The boy did promise and he remembered doing so, but despite Derrick's warnings, his father had never done anything to hurt him.

Besides...No one was evil enough to poison chocolate. Eric decided, talking himself into voiding his suspicions.

Thus, he ran toward the chocolate bar happily.

"Thanks!" He exclaimed as he took it with both hands and pulled it towards him.

He reveled in the sight of the treat for a moment.

"Well, aren't you going to try it?" Dr. Krone urged and when the boy looked at him with a hint of wonderment, he hastily defended his urgency. "I'm simply curious about how it tastes. It's supposedly the best..."

Satisfied with the answer, Eric tore the top off of the wrapper and inhaled the sweet scent of cocoa. There was another, more pungent scent as well, but Eric ignored it.

After all, he couldn't expect it to be exactly like the chocolate he was used to. It was foreign.

Dr. Krone looked on expectantly as Eric prepared to take a large bite.

However, before he could chomp down on the morsel, there was a loud crack, like a door was being kicked down, followed by Derrick's panicked voice echoing through the hall.

"Eric!"

The boy froze, feeling as though he was caught doing something wrong and turned to see his brother racing frantically down the stairs.

"What's the matter? Eat the chocolate. Your brother is jealous, that's all. Don't you trust me?" His father was speaking fast as the boy's eyes darted back and forth between him and his brother.

"No! Don't eat it!" Derrick screamed, racing towards them.

Wide-eyed and afraid, Eric dropped the chocolate bar and backed away, at about the same time Derrick reached him.

Throwing himself between his little brother and his father, Derrick's eyes narrowed.

"I didn't eat it!" Eric insisted, cowering behind Derrick as Dr. Krone's eyes ignited with fury.

Quickly, Derrick scooped up the chocolate and pitched it into the roaring fire.

The fire roared as it licked its chops after consuming the morsel, as though looking for more.

A pungent stench and a burst of flames belching out of the fireplace confirmed Derrick's fears.

Dr. Krone immediately became enraged. He jumped to his feet and stomped towards them.

Now, more concerned than ever about his brother's safety, Derrick pushed Eric behind him and backed away as his father ran at him.

"How could you?" Derrick demanded, genuinely horrified by the elder man's actions. "I have done everything you have asked of me." He narrowed his eyes as his fists balled, taking a defiant stance. "We had a deal!"

Dr. Krone growled, baring his teeth, like the animal that Derrick knew all too well that his father truly was. Hastening his step, Dr. Krone thrust his arm upwards, violently backhanding his son for his perceived transgressions.

Derrick tried to block the blow, but the force of the man's fury was far too much for the eight-year-old to shield. He was instantly knocked off his feet and shot to the side, sliding to a halt merely inches from the blazing, raging inferno.

Immediately, the boy recovered, fearing far more for the safety of his little brother more than any pain his father could inflict on him directly.

Eric screamed his brother's name and tried to get to him, but Dr. Krone shoved him backward when the child got too close.

"Leave him!" His father boomed, watching as the child fell backward.

"Stop it!" Derrick yelled, thrusting himself forward and grabbing ahold of his father's jacket.

Instantly, Dr. Krone whipped around and swung at him again. The boy ducked this time, but stumbled back, closer to the encompassing fireplace.

Dr. Krone didn't stop moving towards him. His expression was manic, his eyes deranged.

Derrick wasn't sure if his father had finally lost the last sliver of sanity, or if he was putting on an outraged act in order to scare him.

Either way, though, he realized it didn't much matter. His father had homicide on his mind and that was the extent of what truly mattered. The only thing that he was sure of was that he needed to ensure, from now on, that he remained the focus of Dr. Krone's contempt.

"You're a backstabbing bastard!" Derrick hissed, catching himself and suddenly ceasing to back up.

Instead, he puffed out his chest and stood tall, defiantly against him.

Dr. Krone's eyes narrowed and his thin face reddened with contempt.

"How dare you!" He growled, attempting to hit him again.

Derrick ducked but lost his footing. Dr. Krone caught him, by the front of his shirt and pushed him until his back was flush against the flames roaring egregiously inside the gaudy hearth.

The flames licked at the boy's back, stinging him unmercifully. He wriggled, trying to get out of the ironclad hold the man held on him, but it was to no avail.

When he realized that he was unable to move, he locked onto his father's arms with both hands and resorted to showcasing his bravado. In an effort not to relay any discomfort, he mashed his teeth and glowered up at his father.

His expression was unwavering. He snarled at him to keep from screaming out.

Dr. Krone chided his attempt to ignore the pain, pushing him further into the fire.

Derrick continued to defy his father.

Behind him, he heard his brother screaming for his father to let him go.

Out of the corner of his eye, he saw Eric run up to his father and grab ahold of his suit jacket.

He tugged it frantically, tears streaming down his face.

"Stop it!" Eric screeched as Dr. Krone spun around, throwing Derrick to the side.

Derrick stumbled back before he caught himself against the brick of the flue. He screamed when he couldn't push himself back quick enough and his hand hissed as it singed.

However, when he watched his father grab ahold of Eric, hoisting him up, off of his feet, looking as though he had every intention of turning his anger on him, Derrick no longer cared about his burning hand.

He shoved himself away from the fire and leaped onto his father's back. Holding on tightly, he clenched his fist and swung it around, catching Dr. Krone in the throat.

He gasped and choked, releasing Eric in order to coddle his throat.

"Run!" Derrick commanded as he wrapped his arm around his father's injured throat and yanked back as hard as he possibly could.

Once again, Dr. Krone let out a wailing, choking moan and reared back, slamming Derrick against the wall.

Using the wall to weaken him, he grabbed his arm and slung the boy over his shoulder, slamming him onto the floor.

Dazed, Derrick was unprepared for the haste of his father's reaction.

Dr. Krone shot his hand forward, closed his fist around his throat and dragged his son up until he could no longer touch the ground.

The moment Derrick's airway was cut off, he gasped and started to kick. He panicked, clawing at his father's hand, trying to free himself from his clutch.

"You worthless little shit!" Dr. Krone screamed, shaking him unmercifully. "I am going to make your life a living hell...and your brother's too."

"I'm sorry!" Derrick choked, trying to gasp for air. "Please...I didn't mean it...I just didn't want you to hurt him."

Soon, the pressure in Derrick's head started to throb unmercifully. With each moment that passed, the more panicked he became.

He tried to fight. He kicked his legs and swayed back and forth, desperately gripping at his father's hand, trying with unbridled desperation to loosen the hold Dr. Krone held on him.

The oxygen he was able to siphon from the minimal access he had to his airway was rapidly depleting. He choked and sputtered, gagging repeatedly as black spots erupted in his vision.

"Please..." He appealed with the last of his remaining breath, even though he knew that it would do no good. If Dr. Krone wished for this to be Derrick's final night, he knew from experience that the usual familial bonds would pose no bearing on his decision.

Blood or otherwise humanistic allegiances were mere pawns, which he routinely used to coerce others. Dr. Krone himself was not bound by such benevolent idiosyncrasies.

"What's the matter? Do you fear death?" Dr. Krone taunted, knowing his son no longer had the breath to answer him. "Do you fear the darkness from which you emerged, because you should." His smirk widened as his eyes glistened with a certain barrage of accomplishment.

Derrick could feel himself slowly losing consciousness. Eventually, the urge to fight was underwhelming, compared to the ease of surrender.

Eventually, he realized that he would have liked nothing more than to welcome the nothingness that threatened to overtake him.

The more his lungs failed him, the burning increasing unmercifully with every failed breath, the easier, he found, it would be to give in.

However, he knew that his incapacitation would leave his brother vulnerable to Dr. Krone's homicidal intentions, so he kept fighting. He refused to leave his brother, with no one to protect him.

After all, even at the age of eight, he had figured out his mother's true intentions had nothing to do with her sons' welfare and they had no other family. That left only Derrick to protect his brother, not only from his father but also from the rest of the world. There were things about Derrick and his brother that no one seemed to understand; they were special, in a way and their innate talents were of great interest to their father.

Derrick was sure that Dr. Krone was studying him. That was why he hadn't killed either of them yet.

It was for these reasons as well as the innate drive to survive, that Derrick refused to accept the promise of an easier way out.

He continued to kick his feet, even though he knew that the movement was futile as he glowered back into his father's eyes; taunting him. Daring him to go through with the kill.

Unfortunately, what he saw staring back at him in those cold, soulless hazel eyes was daunting. It was obvious that the deliberation between letting him live and finally finishing him off was a source of serious contemplation.

Derrick was sure that there was no moral dilemma, but he was well aware of the academic disadvantage of his death.

His analytical mind, which was almost metaphysically advanced, provided his father, not only with a test-subject but also a practical source of resources for otherwise difficult operations.

For years now, Dr. Krone had studied his son's advanced abilities and utilized them to their limits to benefit his illegal dealings. Derrick didn't like being used but he was pleased to be useful' it certainly had its advantages when it came to keeping Eric safe.

However, tonight's attack was the result of what Dr. Krone deemed as Derrick's resistance to help him achieve his unruly goals.

Their task had nearly failed because Derrick had hesitated.

Usually, he wasn't compelled to work in the field with his father, but due to special circumstances and time restraints, he was far more involved than he ever wanted to be. He didn't like the idea of this mission in particular because he knew that his direct involvement would be the reason a lot of people got hurt.

He had told himself that his sense of morality didn't matter, that his brother's life was far more important, but when it finally came down to the last crucial seconds, he had a stroke of conscience. He knew that he only had a few moments to crack the code and gain the information that his father sought, but his guilt over what he was doing took hold, suddenly and without warning.

Of course, his wavering didn't last long, but it was enough time for Dr. Krone to notice.

Thus, Derrick knew that there would be some kind of retaliation. There always was.

Yet, he would never have thought that the punishment would come so swiftly. He barely had any time to prepare before he found himself drowning in the middle of an intensely volatile situation.

Eventually, despite Derrick's best efforts to remain conscious, he felt sleep consume him.

His pain was dissipating. Although he tried to stop it, his fortitude seemed to be to no avail.

Regardless, he continued to cling to the terrible sensations of dying, simply to remind him that he was alive.

However, the more he tried to struggle, which disconnected him further from reality, the more he knew what a losing battle he was fighting.

Soon, he knew that he would lose all sense in reality and become a figment of the past.

Yet, before that happened fully, he felt his feet skid back, against the bricks of the fireplace.

Although he no longer had use of his legs, the sharp sting that reverberated through his brain helped him regain some semblance of consciousness.

Unfortunately, the moment he did was the exact moment that he realized he was once again being held against the fire.

The flames licked his back, scorching it without mercy.

Trying to scream out, he choked, coming to the conclusion that he was still unable to breathe.

Once more, he attempted to wriggle out of his father's grasp but was now far too weak to fight back.

With the flames threatening to engulf him and his airway still completely cut off, Derrick now had no other choice but to yearn for an end to the torment.

He didn't want to die, but his hopeless position caused him to yearn for an end. He had fought for too long. He had built up too much fear and endured too much heartache.

Derrick knew that he could no longer be responsible for what happened to him or anyone else. He was tired of caring. All he wanted to do was fall into the clutches of death and hope that Hell was more tolerable than his life.

At exactly the moment he was willing to allow himself to fall fully into the darkness, though, he felt himself be torn away from the flames and thrown onto the ground.

"I'm not going to kill you..." He heard his father assure before the world finally went completely black.

Little did Derrick know that this was only the beginning...

Chapter 1

Derrick awoke to the stream of sunlight, beckoning from behind the blinds. A deep breath drew in the familiar, welcoming scent of what remained of his fiancée's perfume as she slept soundly in his arms. Instinctively, he hugged her tighter, pulling her closer to him. He grinned as his nose nuzzled through her long, blond hair.

He breathed in again, now able to detect the far more intimate aroma of her soft, sensual, alabaster skin.

Feeling him moving against her, she wriggled closer, giggling and turning her body towards him.

His lips rested against her shoulder as he adjusted to her repositioning as a coy simper spread across her lips.

Her eyes remained lightly closed, but he watched as they danced in thought behind her long lashes.

She too breathed in deeply, her expression brightening as she exhaled.

"Good morning..." Lily grinned, her emerald eyes fluttering opened and immediately searching for Derrick.

His gaze met hers with tenderness.

Lily's hand rose up to meet his face, stroking down his cheek before she arched herself up and pressed her lips firmly against his.

The familiar, yet infinitely alluring taste of her enticed him and when she sat up further turning towards him, he allowed her kiss to follow him back down onto the bed.

As her tongue slid between his teeth and her arms wrapped up, around his neck, he grinned behind the caress of her lips. Wrapping his arms around her securely, he drew her closer to him as her shimmering hair spilled all around him.

The warmth of her skin against his as their legs intertwined was intoxicating.

Closing his eyes, he tilted his head to deepen the kiss. Fervently, Lily reacted, pressing her bosom up against his chest, rocking herself up and down against him.

Derrick groaned as he felt himself pulse against her with ardor exhilaration.

Now, it was Lily that moaned, pulling back from him in a coy, seductive manner.

Her long thin fingers ran up his arms and slowly slid down his chest, expertly tracing each concave that fused together to create a taut weaving, fluid course of chiseled muscle.

He pulled in a deep, elated breath as his eyes followed her hands back to where she was straddling him.

His eye caught the glint of the diamond proudly adorning her ring finger and he wondered how he could've possibly gotten so lucky.

Once her hands glided up, against the overhang of his t-shirt, which was practically falling off the shoulder of her small frame, she paused. Her eyes illuminated with temptation. Raising one eyebrow, the corner of her mouth curled upwards in a teasing manner.

Derrick returned the expression as his eyes grazed over her bodice. Even though the excess material of the t-shirt, he could make out her salacious, firm shape.

Enticed, his heart raced in his chest and his blood pumped furiously in his veins.

He felt her pressing, kneading herself against him and he craved the feeling of being inside of her; All of her.

Derrick swallowed hard, feeling the pulsing in his groin intensify with every new thought about what lay beyond the t-shirt and skimpy underwear that now rode, provokingly overtop of him.

Mind, body, and soul, Lily was the most beautiful, unique woman he had ever met.

He had absolutely no idea why she had chosen him, but he certainly wasn't going to overthink it.

After teasing him for a moment longer, she crossed her arms over her stomach and easily tugged the oversized t-shirt over her head.

His eyes outlined her curves, mesmerized by her voluptuous bosom as her gorgeous locks of hair rained down over her bodice.

With a quick flick of her head, however, her curls hastily slid behind her shoulders, leaving him a complete view of her captivating presence.

Once again, his eyes scoured her body as his arms ran up, to wrap around her waist.

Derrick drew her into him and she lowered herself down so that her now brazenly revealed mounds of feminine allure pressed against his chest.

With a growl of arousal, Derrick reclaimed her mouth, his curious tongue wandering between her parted, pulsing lips.

As the couple drew life and breath from one another, Derrick's fingers combed through her hair, brushing it out of her face, while his other hand slid down the side of her, towards her panties.

Pressing herself down against him further, she invited a deepened kiss as she eased over to the side, tugging Derrick on top of her.

Once he was gazing down at her, he brought his head closer to her and pressed his lips against hers.

However, after gathering a quick taste of her, his mouth traveled over to the corner of hers, and his slow sensual caresses continued a gradual descent, down her neck, towards her breast.

As he moved, he heard Lily moan. Her hands traced up and down his arms as her body opened herself up to him. She tipped her head back and closed her eyes as his path sunk into the valley between her breasts.

At the same time, Derrick's hands coursed down either side of Lily, until he reached her pelvis. When he did, he easily hooked onto the thin string of her panties and slid them off, pulling himself back as he did so.

Watching him discard his own remnants of clothing before returning to her, Lily's eyes grew ravenous with passion.

Leaning back into her, his hands rose up her legs, towards her thighs, but with a shudder of excitement, she reached up and pulled him towards her, positioning him right between her legs.

Immediately, he felt her throbbing, moist sheath as her pelvis rose up against him.

"Oh..." She groaned as their mutual, unbridled need melded.

Her breathing increased as he stroked his pulsating manhood up, against her.

Running his hands back up her torso, he curved his hands around her flushed, firm, supple breasts.

Feeling the rosebud of each blossom into a stiffened peak in his hand, he brought them up and teased them with a tantalizing flick of his tongue.

Lily gasped loudly and quivered with delight as her legs instinctively wrapped around him, compelling him to move closer to her. At the same time, she grasped his arms, almost desperately and arched her back, insinuating that she was ready for him.

He felt a sly grin cross his features at her reaction and after another tantalizing sweep of his firm shaft, he penetrated the veil.

Lily moaned appreciatively as he embedded himself inside of her.

"Oh...God, I love you..." She insisted as the two of them automatically eased into a lovemaking tempo that caused them both to shudder with intensifying carnal desire.

Their cadence was perfected, desired and entrancing.

As Lily writhed beneath him, Derrick was consumed in an overpowering sense of magnificence.

The two continued to rocket towards their climax, their fervid touches and the intertwining of their bodies dramatically enhanced their ascension.

The sound of their mutual panting breaths, shallow and fast filled the room, but the couple had been transported to a world all their own.

In that moment, all that mattered was the feel of their skin, pressing against one another and the sensations wrought from their oneness.

With the progression of their lovemaking, Derrick and Lily increased the speed of their thrusts until they were both testing their endurance.

"Oh...Yes..." Lily exclaimed breathlessly, her grasp tightening around Derrick's arm to keep up with their pace. "Yes...Don't stop...Don't stop..."

Shutting her eyes tightly, her amative moans grew more intense, coinciding with the increase in emotion that was rising inside Derrick.

Pulsating desire coursed through them. Aching, pining rapture consumed them until finally, the glorious moment of release washed over them both.

Lily closed her eyes and pulled herself close to Derrick while his blissful eruption filled her.

As Lily whined with fulfillment as her excitement burned to a cinder and her body convulsed around him, Derrick groaned in delightful agony.

The moment the sensations tapered off into a pleasured consummation, Derrick felt entirely drained but indescribably happy.

He had never thought that his life would ever amount to anything, but while growing up, he was sure of it.

Yet, over the past three years, through the life that he was building with Lily, he had everything he had ever wanted and so much more.

Chapter 2

Lily slid Derrick's coffee across the counter, towards him with a grin before hunching over her own cup and bringing it up to her lips to take a sip.

"Thank you..." He returned the smile, grabbing the cup. Noticing the unusual quiet, though, he narrowed his eyes and spoke before taking a sip. "Is Eva up yet?"

Lily chuckled and shook her head, but didn't have a moment to respond before, as though on cue, the sound of small feet came tearing down the hallway.

"Mommy! Daddy! I'm awake!" The three-year-old announced, her hazel eyes lighting up and her blond curls bouncing wildly as she barreled towards them.

Lily laughed.

"Good morning, Eva..." Lily responded as Derrick caught her mid-stride.

"Intercepted..." He called as he spun her around and she giggled.

"How did you sleep?" Lily asked when they stopped.

"Okay..." Her shoulders rose and lowered as though she wasn't being completely honest.

"What's the matter?" Derrick asked. "Are you still having those dreams? The one about the ghost?"

She pouted and nodded.

"The ghost takes me to different places. He's not mean or anything, but I'm tired. I want to sleep. I don't want to go anywhere." She insisted.

"Eva, sweetie, it's only a dream." Lily insisted, with an understanding tone.

"Yeah, so just enjoy the adventure," Derrick responded, trying to be positive. "Wherever you go, always remember, you can always come home and wake up in your own bed."

"I know." She replied, but the dream seemed to bother her more than it should.

Being that Eva's intelligence was extremely high, her imagination ran away from her often.

However, Derrick couldn't help but think that there was something more to her dreams. After all, he and Eric had special abilities. It wasn't unreasonable to believe that Eva had some kind of gift as well.

Yet, even though he tried, he could never find any correlation between the dreams or the places she goes with *the ghost* and reality. Still, he wasn't about to rule anything out. If she did have an ability, he wanted to find out what it was before anyone else did.

Lily, who knew about their specialties as well had questioned Derrick a few times about their daughter as well, but the conversations never yielded any results.

As Lily placed breakfast on the table, the three of them sat down to eat.

"So, what do you girls have planned for today?" Derrick asked, his eyes passing between Eva and Lily.

"We're going to the park!" Eva burst out with excitement. "Guess what? I can go on the big swings, all by myself."

"Oh yeah?" He asked even though Lily had texted him pictures the day before, too proud to wait to even give Eva the chance to tell him herself.

"Yeah. None of my other friends can do that. They all have to be pushed...If they can even get on the swing." She rolled her eyes and chuckled.

"Mommy..." Eva called, staring at Lily with wide eyes as she changed the subject abruptly.

"Yes, sweetie?"

"Can I go to school?"

"You do go to school." She insisted, shooting Derrick a look that told him this wasn't the first, second, or third time they've had this conversation.

"No. Not pre-school. I know everything..." Her eyes grew even wider as she dramatized her response. "Seriously. Ev-ry-thing!"

Derrick tried to hide his smirk but failed, gaining a disapproving glower from Lily.

"I know, Eva, but you're not old enough. You're only three."

"In two years, I could have solved world problems...Instead, I'll be stuck playing with blocks." She huffed. "It's holdin' me back!"

At this, Derrick couldn't help laughing.

"I think you've been watching too much daytime TV."

"Yeah...She absorbs everything." Lily agreed.

"Well, if I could absorb how to read, or cool stuff about dinosaurs, maybe it'd be more fun."

"I could teach you to read," Lily replied. "And I'm sure your dad could teach you about dinosaurs."

"Great!" She insisted, sounding genuine, before almost immediately changing her tone as she came to another conclusion. "But then what am I going to school for?"

"You have friends at school." Derrick tried.

"Garret's favorite thing to do is eat glue and all Jessie cares about is Barbie dolls and playing games on the iPad. Which, she's bad at, by the way."

"I'm sorry..." Derrick answered, trying not to sound as amused as he was. "What about that girl, Tara?"

"She's the reason I want to go to Kindergarten." Eva insisted. "She's five. I can talk to her."

"I see."

"Daddy gets it!"

"What?" Derrick insisted, wondering how this turned around on him. "What do I get?" He looked playfully between Eva and Lily. "I don't get anything. Don't pull me into this."

"Didn't you say that you and Uncle Eric were always better at school than everyone else?" Eva eyed her father seriously, trying to prove her point.

"Yeah, but we enjoyed the fact that it was easy. We didn't have ambition."

"Derrick!" Lily scolded. "Don't tell her that!"

"But...Of course, I want you to do anything you set your mind too." He added cautiously, watching Lily out of the corner of his eye, trying to dig himself out of trouble. When he couldn't tell whether he was gaining any brownie points or not, he gave up and spoke honestly to Eva. "I wish I had your drive when I was...any age." He smirked. "I am so proud of you for everything that you do and I don't want you to give up. If you really want to be challenged and you can't get it through school, we'll find something...a club or something that you can join."

"That sounds like a good idea!" Lily chimed in before glancing at the clock. "Speaking of which, you need to go get your shoes on, or you're going to be late for your playdate at the park."

"Oh, yeah!" Eva's eyes lit up again as though the conversation had momentarily distracted her from her plans.

"Don't forget the glue!" Derrick called after her, earning another giggle, as Lily rolled her eyes.

Once she was sure she was in her room, Lily sauntered over to Derrick and lowered her voice.

"Do you think she's okay?"

Realizing she was genuinely worried, he wrapped his arms around her waist and pulled her closer to him.

"Yeah. I think she's great."

"I'm worried...With the nightmares and having trouble at school..."

Derrick chuckled.

"Lily, sweetie, our daughter is smarter than everyone else in school. That's not having trouble. That's being bored and trust me, I'd rather her be bored then struggling. It's fine. She wants to learn. She's excited to learn...That's wonderful." He squeezed her hand reassuringly. "And besides, she basically just equated solving the world's problems to her learning to read and studying dinosaurs." He shook his head in a teasing manner. "If only the world was that simple."

"Oh, but it is." She mused, leaning in to brush a soft kiss on his lips. "At least, your daughter seems to think so..." She teased as she pulled away.

"She thinks she knows everything." He retorted playfully.

"I wonder where she learned that from?" Her eyebrows raised in a mocking, accusatory manner.

"I can't help it." His shoulders rose and fell. "You know, it's not an easy burden. Sometimes knowing everything has its downfalls." He grinned.

Lily rolled her eyes and shook her head.

"So, what are you doing today?" She asked as she turned around and started to clean up the kitchen.

"I have a few predictions I would like to iron out...a couple calls to make and...I don't know. I'm hoping I'll be done by one."

Lily knew that he made his living manipulating the stock market. His analytical mind made him quite good at figuring out the ebb and flow of Wall Street.

She didn't mind what he did for a living, but she also didn't ask many questions.

It wasn't that Derrick had anything to hide; especially from her, but he also didn't mind the idea that she didn't need to know everything. What he did was often extremely hard to understand and, whether or not he could explain it in a way that she would understand was irrelevant. He simply didn't want to have to explain everything he did and the decisions he made.

Due to his business practices, they did have money. He could've afforded any number of houses and practically anything that any of them desired.

However, besides the fact that he simply wasn't that way, he also didn't want to draw attention to them. If he flaunted his money, his father, if he were still alive, or any number of agencies would be banging down his door, trying to get their cut.

Derrick didn't want that. He simply wanted to be comfortable and live out his life with the woman he loved and their daughter.

Lily had always agreed.

"Great!" She exclaimed. "If you are done in time, maybe we can do something this afternoon."

"Sure. That'd be great."

"Mommy! I'm ready!" Eva called as she bustled down the hall. Her shoes clopping loudly as she ran.

"Okay…" Lily grinned as she watched Eva reappear in the room. "I'm ready too." She leaned in and kissed Derrick again before turning towards the door.

"Bye, Daddy…" Eva exclaimed, leaping up, into his arms to give him a hug and kiss him goodbye.

"Bye, girls…Love you." He called after them, watching Eva take her mother's hand.

"We love you too!" Lily called over her shoulder as they walked towards the door.

When the two of them left that day, Derrick had absolutely no idea that this was one of the last, precious moments of normalcy and genuine happiness that he had left.

Chapter 3

After his family left the house, Derrick refilled his coffee and moved into the office that was conveniently placed fairly far out of the way from the main living space of the house.

It was a quiet place, where Derrick could work in peace.

Knowing that he was pressed for time, as soon as he was settled, he started to make his way through the list of tasks he had rattled off to Lily earlier.

Throughout that time, he received a few text messages from his fiancée with pictures of Eva playing at the park and eventually going for pizza with the same people they went to the park with.

It was a welcome distraction from the business he needed to attend to, but even with all of that, he managed to finish right around the time he was supposed to.

Although, one text message he received immediately incited worry and a sense of panic that he hadn't felt in years.

When Eric's name showed up on his phone, he didn't think much of it at first and continued the final conversation he needed to have before he was done with business for the day.

Therefore, he didn't read it until after he was finished with the phone call.

Krone's here. SOS.

"What?" Derrick demanded, immediately trying to call his brother back. To his horror, the call went right to voicemail. "What's going on? I'm coming over now. Please...Call me back. Let me know you're okay."

By the time he ended the phone call, Derrick's heart was racing. Immediately, he felt nauseous.

Part of him knew that he should've expected this, but part of him was far more shocked than he knew he should be.

After shooting off a text message to Lily, telling her that something was going on with Eric and he had to go over there to take care of it, he left the house.

Immediately, the phone rang.

"What's going on? Is he okay?" Lily asked when Derrick answered.

He started up his truck before he responded.

"I don't know. He says he's in some kind of trouble." He explained, not wanting to worry her. Mentioning his father would take far more explaining than he could handle at the moment, so he decided against it. "Are you on your way home?"

"Yeah. Eva's asleep." She chuckled. "Between the park and pizza, she didn't stand a chance."

"Okay. Great." He answered, only half listening. "Just do me a favor and lock the doors when you get home."

Immediately, her voice morphed into grave concern.

"Sure, but...why? Derrick, what's going on?"

"Hopefully nothing. Like I said, I got a weird text from Eric. It's..." He sighed and rolled his eyes, but decided to elaborate. "It's about my father..."

"Oh..." Lily sounded surprised.

"But it doesn't matter. I'm taking care of it. I just want you two to be safe. I'll be home as soon as I can."

"Okay..." She replied, sounding slightly on edge. "Please let me know what's going on when you know more, okay?"

"I will. I promise." He assured. "I love you."

"I love you too." She responded. "If there's anything I can do to help..."

"Just lock the doors. Don't let anyone inside. I'll call you as soon as I can."

"Thank you." She replied, now making an effort to sound positive.

Upon hanging up with Lily, he tried to call Eric again, but the call still went straight to his voicemail, which heightened Derrick's fear.

Eric lived in the same house the two of them had grown up in, along with their mother, when she bothered to come home.

Karen loved her trips and vacations. She also liked her other men. Although still technically still married to Krone, their open relationship became nonexistent when he disappeared.

She moved on with her life, leaving her sons to fend for themselves.

While they never wanted for food or shelter, an adult presence was nearly nonexistent.

Therefore, at fifteen, Eric was often left to his own devices.

Derrick and Lily had offered to let him have the spare bedroom at their house, but by that point, he was far to use to practically living on his own.

He liked his privacy and was comfortable with the life he had built without anyone looking over his shoulder.

The drive to his mother's house took Derrick forty minutes.

At the time he bought his house, he did that purposefully. The only connection he still considered himself having to that house was Eric's residence and he encouraged his older brother to run as far away as he could.

Still, he didn't want to be too far away, in case an emergency ever did arise.

Now, however, that forty-minute drive felt like an eternity.

Throughout the trip, he continued to try to call Eric, to no avail.

Thus, when he finally did pull into the long, pristinely manicured driveway, he barely stopped the truck before leaping out.

Derrick rushed into his mother's house, past the fireplace that held so many rotten memories and up the stairs towards his brother's room.

As he ran, he did pick up on the fact that there didn't seem to be anything amiss in the house.

Yet, he knew from experience that with his father, it was sometimes impossible to tell.

Therefore, once he reached the room that his brother had inhabited since they were both children, he barged inside without a second thought.

Instantly, Eric jumped up and spun around, glaring at the intruder, already in a stance, ready to fight.

When he saw it was his brother, he stopped and backed up before he ripped the headphones out of his ears and glared at him.

"What the hell is wrong with you?" After a moment, he quickly amended his statement as he demanded. "Are you okay?"

Derrick looked around the room, still waiting for some kind of threat to be lurking, before his eyes met his brother's and he hissed, "You've got to be kidding me. What's wrong with me? What the hell's the matter with you?"

"What did I do?"

Noticing that he seemed genuinely confused, Derrick's tone softened into more of a question instead of a demand.

"Didn't you say that you needed help, that you were in trouble? That Krone was here?"

Eric searched the room for an answer while he tried to figure out what was going on.

"No. I'm fine. I've been here, alone all day." He narrowed his eyes, his voice quickly falling into a concerned tone. "Is everything alright with you?"

Derrick yanked his phone out of his pocket and shoved it towards Eric, showing him the text.

"You didn't send this?"

His eyes searched over the text and his face scrunched up with complete misunderstanding.

"No. I didn't."

"Why is your phone off? I called you..."

"It's not." Eric pulled his phone out of his pocket and showed his brother that as far as he knew, he hadn't missed anything.

At first, Derrick was confused, but soon, that confusion turned to terror.

He gasped as his worst fears were realized.

"He wanted me out of the house." Derrick surmised.

"What?" Eric still hadn't caught on. "Who? Krone? Why?"

"No..." His eyes grew wide as his breath hastened. He was no longer hearing a word Eric said. His mind was racing and all he could think about was the length of time it would take him to get back to his house. "Oh, God...I've got to get home!" He yelled and without any further explanation, he turned around and bolted out of the house.

Derrick heard Eric running up behind him, trying to make sense of the strange encounter, but he didn't stop for a moment, fearing that it was already too late.

In one hasty motion, he threw opened the door of his truck and slid inside. Jamming the key in the ignition, he took off as soon as he was able.

His heart was pounding and his head hurt from the pressure of his anxiety, but all that mattered to him at that moment was getting home.

Going into this, he had a bad feeling, boiling in the pit of his stomach, but he ignored it. He knew that he would have never forgiven himself if he hadn't responded to the text, but by doing so, he had left everyone he cared about completely exposed.

The ride back to the house seemed to pass in a blur.

He tried to call Lily, but the vague memory of hearing her answering machine pick up only heightened his fears. His mind was racing, hoping and praying that he was overreacting.

He didn't leave a message. Instead, he threw the phone into the passenger's seat and hastened his pace.

However, from the moment that he pulled into the driveway, he had an awful feeling that he had made a grave mistake.

The adrenaline that pumped through him caused his ears to feel as though they were pulsing. He knew that he had to think clearly, but his concern for what might have happened in his absence clouded his judgment.

As he yanked the keys out of the ignition of his old pickup truck and rushed through the yard, towards his front door, the feeling only intensified.

Chapter 4

When Lily saw Derrick's name come up on the screen of her phone, she breathed a silent sigh of relief. "Hey, is everything alright with your brother?"

A bold quip of a snicker erupted in her ear, but the voice on the other end of the phone said nothing more.

"Hello?" She responded, looking at her phone with confusion which left her heart thudding with nervousness when she realized that whoever was on the other end was either calling from her fiancé's phone or at least making it appear that way. "Who is this?" She demanded.

All that she received was a mocking sneer.

"Where's Derrick? Put him on the phone...This isn't funny..." Despite her words, however, Lily's last hope was that this was some kind of joke.

"Oh, I assure you, my dear, there is no deception." The man spoke for the first time, commanding a strong, proper, yet raspy voice into her ear. "He can't come to the phone right now, but I'm sure he would send his best...That is if he knew that we were having this conversation."

Lily felt her stomach churn as she exhaled nervously. "Where is he?" She demanded, glancing around the house and making a quick sprint for Eva's room.

"That actually doesn't matter right now. What does matter is that I am extremely interested in meeting you...and that little bundle of joy that you brought home."

"Stop this! I'm gonna call the police." Lily hissed, reaching the baby's room and sending up a silent prayer that the child seemed to be perfectly safe inside her bed.

Without stopping, Lily rushed over to the opposite side of the room to ensure that her daughter was resting peacefully. She felt her breath once again release in a relieved fashion, resisting the urge to pick Eva up, not wanting to wake her daughter, or alarm her unnecessarily.

However, this time, a dark, malicious cackle came over the phone before the man responded in a dementedly amused, repugnant manner. "Lily, I hate to be the one to break it to you..."

When the voice paused, Lily stopped, realizing with horror that the words were not only being spoken through the phone.

There was a slight echo before the line went dead, but the voice remained. "But I'm already here."

Lily felt the hair stand up on the back of her neck and she whipped around, doing her best to shield the bed from the intruder and remain calm. She gasped and backed up, eyes wide and fearful as a slim man slunk out of the shadows.

His thin lips curled devilishly into a grin and his eyes were ignited by her surprise.

"Who are you?" She demanded. "What are you doing in my house?"

The man laughed as he produced a pistol from inside his azure suit-jacket and pointed it at her.

"If Derrick hasn't felt the need to warn you about me, then he must not care for you or that child much at all."

Seeing the gun caused Lily to freeze. She gasped, raising her hands cooperatively and dropping her cell phone.

"Take whatever you want...Just leave the baby alone."

A hushed, humored ripple coiled from deep within the man's gut while his expression gleamed.

"I can't do that. After all, the baby is the reason I'm here."

Chapter 5

Once inside the house, an eerie sense of calm scoured the rooms. Derrick was sure that something wasn't right.

"Lily?" He called, eyeing the living room which seemed fairly undisturbed. However, the fact that there was no answer was completely unsettling. "Lily, is everything okay?" He asked again with caution.

He remembered noticing that her car was still parked in the driveway, but that didn't necessarily mean that she was home.

Derrick tried to force himself to remember that.

After all, if there was nothing wrong, he didn't want to alarm his fiancée, but if there was, he didn't want to be the one surprised.

When he listened again, he thought he heard rustling in the back of the house.

"Eva..." He hissed under his breath and rushed back to the room where his daughter should have been sleeping soundly.

"Lily!" He called, with far more desperation consuming his voice than he intended to portray.

The morbid, harrowing feeling of rot, ate away at his insides. He yearned for relief as he raced down the hall.

He hoped, somewhat naively, that the worry which nearly debilitated him was a product of his overactive imagination; ghosts from a life he had a long time ago, but had taken great pains to escape.

Yet, experience told him that he should know better.

When he reached his daughter's room, he found nothing but Lily's tablet, lying inside the bed. There was a note stuck to the blackened screen.

Hello, Derrick, was all that was written. He recognized the handwriting immediately. He had seen it countless times when he was younger, usually leading him to instructions that would compel him to do something terrible. The sinking feeling in his stomach told him that this note was similar in its intent.

With a shaking hand, he pulled the note off of the screen and set it aside. As he roused the tablet, illuminating it, he hastily typed in the password and gained access.

The screen led him to a video, which appeared to have been filmed from the tablet.

Even before playing the video, Derrick's heart dropped. The still image staring back at him was of Lily, sitting at their kitchen table.

Her hands appeared to be bound behind her and she looked visibly distressed.

Caught slightly off guard by the harrowing image, Derrick stared at it for a moment, before drawing in a choppy breath, in an attempt to prepare himself for watching the video.

Yet, before it even started, Derrick had to resist the urge to chuck the tablet against the wall, simply so that he wouldn't have to endure the sight any longer.

His stomach lurched and he felt sick, but he knew that every moment counted now and he needed to find out what happened to his family.

As he prompted the video to play, he felt his gut wrench as he tried to ignore the ominous sense of hopelessness that plagued him.

The image that he first saw of Lily remained unchanged as the audible sound of video silence signaled the start of Derrick's worst nightmare.

For the first ten seconds, Lily remained still and quiet, as though silently rebelling against her captor's wishes.

"You know..." A chillingly familiar voice exclaimed from the other side of the camera. "In order to get what we want; you don't have to say a word."

Immediately, her expression tightened and her eyes narrowed. He watched the small amount of color in her frightened expression drain from her face and he felt his heartbeat race.

He yearned to comfort her, to help her but knew that he couldn't. An awful flood of guilt and horror overtook him.

"Okay...Okay." She insisted, her pallor growing even more noticeable. "Please..." She winced before looking back at the camera.

Her eyes were glassy, obviously trying to fight back tears. After a long blink and a deep inhale, Lily returned her full attention to the camera.

"Hi, Derrick..." She paused briefly, looked past the camera to those who were coercing her. She bit her lip nervously, as though reacting to something that Derrick couldn't see or hear. She swallowed hard before speaking again. "Please listen carefully, because you'll only be able to see this once."

Her eyes shifted as though she was reading as she spoke, but stopped abruptly, momentarily overcome with emotion. She hastily drew in a quivering breath and shuddered, as though it pained her to follow the directions that she was given.

"This man...he says he's your father...He...He took Eva and I. He wants you to come after us...He threatened to kill me if you don't...I..." Fresh tears suddenly broke through the wall of defense that she was trying to build as she read what she was supposed to say next. Her words halted abruptly and her eyes flickered up, past the camera again and purposefully glowered with a hateful expression.

"If you won't say it, it'll be my pleasure to show him." The voice insisted, breaking into the feed again. "And I can guarantee that will hurt far worse than anything you can say."

After a moment, she swallowed hard and straightened, but returned her gaze to the camera. She closed her eyes and sobbed, shaking her head in a guilty fashion.

Once she composed herself, she opened her eyes again and continued to speak, but it was clear to Derrick that she wasn't reading anymore.

"He wants me to tell you that I don't want to die. He wants me to beg you to save me, but Derrick, please don't come here. He took Eva away. This is just a distraction so he can hide our daughter. Find her...Don't worry about me..." Her eyes grew wide as and she spoke faster, this time genuinely pleading. "He's going to kill me anyway...I don't want you to watch me die...Please...Find Eva..."

With that, the screen went black. The last thing he heard was the sound of a scuffle and an involuntary scream of pain.

Afterward, everything went silent, but the video still wasn't over.

A few seconds after the silence ensued, the voice of Dr. Krone broke through the darkness.

"You can't help your daughter. She is already beyond your reach. Lily, however, might still be able to be saved. Remember, death is the ultimate destination. The journey can be far more harrowing. You know that I can hurt her and in one hour from now, I will."

Derrick felt physically ill. His mind was racing and the fury that coursed through him was unmatched.

Immediately after the video stopped, the picture disappeared and the screen turned black.

A message popped up that informed him the file was unreadable before the entire tablet zapped off.

Derrick closed his eyes, trying to keep his emotions in check.

However, he couldn't get the image of Lily out of his head. It haunted him as he finally gave into the original instinct he had.

With an aggravated growl, he spun around and threw the tablet at the wall, shattering the screen instantly.

"God dammit!" He screamed as he sunk to the ground, burying his head in his hands.

Lily's voice, her fear and her attempt to protect Eva all weighed heavily on him.

Despite Lily's wishes, though, he knew that he couldn't let her die. He needed to try to save them both, or he would never forgive himself.

After a moment, a text came through to his phone. He saw that the number was unknown, but he instantly recognized who it was that sent it.

An address stared back at him.

Derrick knew that Krone was playing a sick and twisted game, but if he had any hope of saving his family, he knew that he had to go along with it.

Chapter 6

When he reached the old, abandoned building, Derrick wasted no time deciding the best way to get inside. Bought years ago by none other than Dr. Krone himself and left to decay when he no longer needed it anymore, Derrick was sure this was the place.

He remembered conducting business there years before and even then, he knew that if he ever had to come back in his lifetime, it would be too soon.

Still, Derrick would have never imagined that when he did return, it would be under these circumstances.

This was, by far, the worst trick Krone had ever played on him; the worst cruelty he had forced him to endure.

As he pulled his truck around the back so that it wouldn't be spotted by anyone passing by, he knew that his only remaining, sliver of hope was that he could provide his father with something he needed.

Unfortunately, having thought, until today, that his father was dead or otherwise removed from his life forever, Derrick had no idea what his father wanted.

Yet, he knew there was nothing he wouldn't do to ensure his family's safety now that Krone had returned.

Derrick figured, as he started to kick in the door, that there was an extremely slim chance he would ever get to return to a normal life with his family.

Even so, if Lily and Eva were safe, he would allow Krone to do whatever he wanted to him for as long as he wanted. He would never raise a question about what he was commanded to do. He would be a good soldier; the best, as long as Krone never did anything to hurt his family again.

When the door burst open, Derrick stepped inside and looked around.

In ten years, the place hadn't changed much.

A thick layer of dust coated the room that was once rented as office space; a front for far more sinister business.

Yet, with a cleaning service and an upgrade in technology, Krone could open right back up.

Untouched, bulky monitors, devoid of all modern conveniences sat in cubicles that hadn't seen a worker in a decade. Pens and pencils, notepads and photocopy paper still sat right where they were needed. Reminders were still pinned to corkboards and there was even a large dry-erase board that detailed the sales goals for the week, a little over a decade ago.

In a way, the untouched, abandoned office was creepy in and of itself.

Of course, Krone never conducted business out here in the open and there was no reason to believe that he would start such a practice now.

So, instead of checking the cubicles, Derrick ran straight to the back. He remembered that there was a supply closet that led into Krone's true purpose for the building.

This portion of the building was crude and, most importantly, soundproof.

As the door closed behind him, he was fairly certain that he heard it lock.

Derrick was on the defensive immediately.

He stopped, his eyes piercing around in the dim factory lighting. He listened for any sign of life but heard nothing.

When he started to cautiously creep forward, Derrick heard his own footsteps rapping softly against the concrete floor.

He looked around, before advancing further.

Much like he remembered it, this hidden portion of the building, which made up the majority of the space, looked innocent enough. It maintained the veneer of a typical storage building.

Pallet racks, lined with what appeared to be product and supplies piled five tiers high and was positioned into aisles that made a maze of the otherwise spacious warehouse.

Ladders, lifts and loading bays sprinkled throughout the workspace. In the prime of this front, at first glance, it would appear that nothing was amiss. Yet, if one were to look closer, they would find that what the workers were moving and compartmentalizing had nothing to do with office supplies.

Everything from drugs to weapons moved through this area at one time. Now, however, Derrick doubted that anything was more than it appeared to be. With no one to watch it, even using it as storage would be far too risky for Krone.

He wasn't sure what he should be looking for. Should he be searching for another terrible clue, leading him on another chase? Or, is this the finale that Krone had planned?

Either way, Derrick knew that it wouldn't be good. He didn't know why he wanted his family, more than simply to hurt him, but something told him that wasn't his primary motivation.

His stomach churned nervously when he thought of what the real reason might be.

However, of all the questions and painstaking questions that loomed in his mind. There was one that stood out among the rest.

Why now?

Still, he realized that none of those questions mattered. Frankly, if it didn't help him get his family back safe, he didn't care why his father did anything.

He had stopped caring about Krone's motives for everything a long time ago.

After all, there was no sanity behind his thought process. It all boiled down to greed or vengeance. Whatever suited Dr. Krone and his ultimate goal was his sole reason for making all of his dastardly decisions.

Carefully, Derrick inched through the main row of shelving, glancing down each aisle and listening keenly for any sign of Lily.

He wanted to call out to her but refrained. He knew that more than likely, it would do no good and would compromise his position far more than he already had by walking around blindly.

The depth of the warehouse seemed to be endless and although his eyes adjusted to the dim lighting rather quickly, he couldn't bring himself to fully trust his surroundings.

Yet, the further he ventured into the bowels of the warehouse, the more anxious he became. The eerie quiet of his surroundings seemed to compound his nervousness. He knew to expect something horrible, but since he didn't know what form the terror would present itself in, his emotions were raw with anticipation.

He tried to force his mind to focus, but everything that could happen distracted him. He knew that he was vulnerable. He had to rely on his instincts, which were running ramped with concern.

Finally, though, he heard something coming from one of the aisles. If he had heard right, he swore that he heard a sigh.

Intrigued by the sudden presence of another person, he whipped around and peered down the narrow corridor.

To his dismay, the depth caused the dim lighten to dull even more until the glow of it only illuminated a cloak of darkness towards what he could only guess was the end.

He turned down the aisle, moving with care and caution.

Again, he wanted to call out to Lily, in the hopes of assuring her everything would be alright, but he thought better of it.

When he reached what he believed was halfway down the aisle, though, he heard another sound. He quickly turned to detect the source of the metal grinding against metal. He watched the large shelf next to him sway before tipping towards him.

Derrick tried to leap out of the way, but the shelf was too large. Even before it smashed into the shelf opposite it, the items that ensured it was top-heavy came tumbling down in a wave of heavy hardware and tools.

When he concluded that there was no true escape from the trap he had walked into, he covered his head and tried to shield himself, but the metallic current of debris bombarded him. He felt different objects pummel him in rapid succession, nearly burying him.

Eventually, though, the attack ceased. In the crucial moment that followed, however, Derrick stood up to assess the damage and was caught in the back of the head by a swinging object. The clang that he felt as it connected with the back of his skull told him that it was likely a bat that hit him.

He tried to fight the sudden black cloud that surrounded him, but as his knees buckled and he fell onto the heap of fallen objects, he couldn't help but succumb.

In an instant, his whole world went dark.

Chapter 7

Derrick's head was pounding when he awoke. His eyes felt like they were going to explode in their sockets and his heart continued to race with fear, even before his mind was able to rationalize the reason behind his anguish.

He felt the blood pumping down the side of his head with each beat of his pulse while the same metallic, crimson taste coated his tongue.

He opened his eyes but found that he was still blind. It took him a moment to realize that part of the pressure that caused his head to ache was due to the blindfold that was wrapped tightly around it.

The sense of panic that he felt soared as he tried to come to grips with what was happening. Behind his skull-shattering headache, his emotions were distraught.

*Lily...Eva...*He thought, regaining consciousness quickly within the concern he held for his family's safety.

However, with the awareness also came the memory of what had happened. The sight of how he was distracted enough to become rendered unconscious plagued him and instantly, his heart thrashed with fear.

Oh God...His mind was frantic and once he regained enough mental power to attempt movement, he leaped forward, in an effort to find the two people he loved most in this world. Yet, his efforts were thwarted almost immediately by a taut, thin rope that bound his hands immovably.

"Derrick?" He heard Lily's voice call in the darkness.

In hearing her, Derrick wasn't sure if he should be happy or absolutely terrified. She seemed so close and yet, he had no way of getting to her.

"Lily..." He breathed as he struggled against the ropes that he now realized bound both his hands and feet. All the while, he tried his best to at least sound as though he was calm. "Are you alright? Did he hurt you?"

"I'm okay..." Lily answered carefully before succumbing to the rush of emotion that was building up inside of her. She sobbed loudly. "But Eva..."

"Where is she?" Derrick demanded, now wildly fighting against the ropes.

"He took her! She's..." Lily stopped short before giving out a long, hurt shudder which coursed hastily into a sob. "I'm so sorry."

"No!" He replied, trying to fight his own emotions while continuing the attempt to reassure her. "It's not your fault...This is all on me. I'm the one who..." With that, reality struck Derrick as well and he heaved a long, pained breath. "Oh God...What have I done? I'm sorry, Lily." Anger coursed through him unmercifully and ire quickly singed deep into his soul.

61

Derrick thrashed with fervor. He felt the wood that ran the length of his body creak and whine, but regardless of what he did, it wouldn't break. Still, he didn't want to act as afraid as he was, even to Lily. He wanted to give her hope. Therefore, when he needed to take a break from fighting the ropes, he composed himself quickly and drew in an assuring breath.

"I swear, Lily. I will get you out of this and I will bring Eva home. I promise."

"I love you." Lily's voice burst out, as though she was afraid she might never be able to say it again.

The sound of her voice, coupled with the dire situation they found themselves in struck him with a feeling akin to a corkscrew being thrust into his chest and wound around with a slow, relentless cadence.

Derrick squeezed his eyes shut and silently sighed, already teetering on a sense of defeat that nearly shattered him.

"And I love you." He replied, trying to draw strength from the statement, but found only failure.

Before she could say anything more, Derrick heard Lily gasp and force herself into a hushed silence.

"Lily?" Derrick called, feeling the new, immense wave of tension that had entered the room.

All he received in response was a shaking, fearful breath.

"How dare you insult her intelligence by naively assuring her you, of all people, will be able to resolve this dreadful situation. Everyone present is already aware of the magnificent deception that statement holds." A terribly familiar voice exclaimed in a mocking tone.

"You son of a bitch." Derrick hissed, once again fighting against his binds with a frenzied, ardor disposition. He wrung his wrists with such a force that he could already feel the skin peeling away, causing every motion to sting.

Yet, Derrick barely noticed. His mind was racing and all he could think about was figuring a way out of this situation for Lily and retrieving his daughter unharmed.

"Yes, she was." He answered. "But for the record, your grandfather was also quite the bastard, in his own right."

Lily trembled again before he heard her shift hastily, as though trying to put distance between herself and a situation that she found absolutely terrifying.

"Derrick..." She cried, instinctively which yet again caused him pain.

"Stop it!" He snarled, still trying to work himself free with all of his might. He felt himself losing complete control, but even though the rage was present, he couldn't free himself enough to unleash it.

How dare he come after his family. There was no reason for it. Both of his sons had left him alone after he disappeared.

"It's okay..." Lily answered instantly, realizing that her inadvertent slip of trepidation had only caused him additional agony. "I'm alright. I'm sorry..."

Derrick could tell that she was trying to keep her voice even, but he recognized the tone. It was the same he had used with her and to his dismay, it wasn't the least bit convincing.

"Oh, come now..." The voice exclaimed in a sharp, castigating tone. After a brief moment, he continued. "You and I both know that you are far from alright."

At this, Derrick sensed someone behind him. Roughly, the blindfold was torn off and he was momentarily dazed and rendered sightless still, by the sudden burst of lighting. Inadvertently squeezing his eyes shut, he turned his head away for a moment, before vigorously turning it back, only to catch a hard right hook that bust opened his lip and left him reeling.

The disorientation had little time to become subdued before he felt a few more blows to his head, each time exploding a thrashing, reverberating pain through his skull. The metallic taste of crimson flowed through his teeth and filled his mouth, but the physical agony was bearable. His body reacted, but his soul was apathetic.

He absorbed the assault, put it out of his mind, decidedly content that his father's sanguinary obsession was, at least for the moment, being spent on him instead of Lily.

It bought him time to think.

However, when he didn't respond appropriately, the pounding in his head worsened. Splintering agony coursed through his mind, distracting him from his thoughts.

Somewhere, beyond the corporal chastisement, Derrick heard his fiancée's pleas for them to stop.

"No!" Lily screamed with such a potency that her voice became almost instantaneously hoarse. "Leave him alone! What is wrong with you? Stop it!"

With each blow, she grew louder.

Derrick wanted to tell her that he was okay. He wished to share his thoughts and preferences with her. However, between the excessive wracking of his brain and the presence of their enemies, there was no way to express that he was happy to endure anything they could muster, so long as their attention was focused on him.

Again, he tried to shut everything out so that he could use the time he was given by their distraction to figure out a way to save his family.

However, the physical torment was weakening him. He found it harder to think with every blow. His outward, superficial anguish, which now consisted of broken bones, countless bruises and an eye that would be swollen shut for days, drained him ruthlessly. He grew violently frustrated with the damage, which caused his body to betray him, despite his efforts to outsmart his restraints.

His heart burned with rage and his blood boiled as he continued to challenge the ropes that rendered him helpless, knowing that he couldn't do anything until he was free. He growled and glowered defiantly at the men who attacked him, snarling jeers at them, trying to endure long enough for him to figure out an advantage.

Alas, with a final blow to the abdomen, which knocked the wind out of him and forced him to recoil as he struggled to retain his composure, the men backed away from him.

The moment he was able to inhale a full breath and stand up straight, although the act of defiance was uncomfortable, he glared at the men surrounding them with a warning. Trying to regain their full attention, he spat out the blood that oozed through his teeth and filled his mouth, aiming for their feet.

"What happened? I'm far from dead, fellas...All you did was piss me off." He jeered in an exasperated tone, trying not to show how difficult it was for him to breathe.

"No..." He heard Lily hiss under her breath in a panic, but he ignored her.

Derrick didn't care what happened to him. He had endured countless forms of torture from the man who stood between him and Lily now. However, anything he could do to him, anything he had done to him, was all practically charitable to even the thought of his family being harmed at his or anyone else's hand.

"I know you're only following orders, but instead, why don't you show the boss you have a set of balls and take another shot at me?"

Once again, Derrick spewed blood in their direction, aiming specifically for his father. He watched as his face distorted into an expression of discontent while the other men shot astounded looks towards their boss.

With a curt flick of his head, the one man balled up his fist took another fury-induced swing at Derrick's face. The other man was soon to follow, continuing to beat him mercilessly.

Each blow caused him to grow weaker. He felt as though his chest was caving in while blood gurgled in his throat. He had the thought that he might choke on it, but he refused to stop breathing.

He didn't mind dying, but he wanted to make sure that Lily and Eva were safe before he allowed himself to surrender to the darkness that was closing in on him, threatening to consume him.

Chapter 8

Lily groveled desperately as she too fought against her own bounds.

"No! Stop it...Please!" She begged.

To Derrick's dismay at the sound of her desperation, the men were ordered to turn their attention away from him.

"It's alright, Lily..." Derrick insisted the moment he was able to regain his breath enough to speak. "I'm fine."

Through his one remaining good eye, he watched Lily turn her attention to him, locking him in her gaze with a horrified expression that made him wonder how bad he actually appeared.

From the throbbing ache that encased his entire body, he could only imagine what his outward appearance portrayed, but that wasn't important to him. What mattered was that the attention of their attackers had returned their focus to Lily and Derrick wanted to change that as soon as possible.

"Again with the falsehoods of the fine idiom. Of course, it's meant to assuage affliction and eliminate doubt, but for one to allow such a colloquialism to shield them from the truth is merely a fool's errand." At that, Derrick felt a strong hand grasp the top of his head and slam it back against the wood, jarring his jumbled skull further.

Derrick heard something crack as an aching burst split through him and he wasn't sure if the sound was the wood or his own head. Gritting his teeth against the blow, he tried not to yell out, although when he opened his eyes, he found he was unable to focus fully.

Lily shrieked in a manner that was quickly overcome by emotion and fresh tears.

"Did you honestly believe he was going to protect you?" He bellowed within a deep throated laugh. Yanking Derrick's head towards him, he glowered into his son's eyes and snickered at his incapacitation.

After a hard, jeering stare, his leer returned to Lily's gaze, mocking her.

"Don't hurt her!" Derrick screamed, fighting his own body now, as well as the ropes that only seemed to dig deeper into his skin with every motion he made. "Return my daughter and let them leave,

unharmed and I'll do anything you want." His voice was forced out, words diving through the free-flowing crimson that continuously filled his mouth, before becoming audible.

Krone simply chuckled and deepened the meaning of the expression he was shooting towards Lily.

"See what the man you love is willing to do, to save you? The lengths to which he would go..." He paused to sneer back at

Derrick before continuing. "I have no doubt that he is telling the truth. He would easily die for you, kill for you even, if it meant that your lives would be spared. He's a monster, really. Unfortunately for you, he only showed you the part of him he knew you would love." His expression turned devilish as his words were spoken with a toxic, derisive potency. "However, when he's stripped down to the bone, you find that it's merely selfishness that drives him."

"No...You don't know anything about him!" Lily hissed as anger now washed through her fear, diluting it, slightly, but was far from removing it completely.

Still, he whipped around to face Derrick, his sharp teeth gleaming and his eyes illuminated with revelation.

"You may claim that you're trying to protect your family...You may have never raised a hand against them, but until you've stood over my dead body, drenched in my blood, you should have known better than to bring anyone you truly cared for into this life. This final, desperate grasp at the last remaining shred of your humanity has manifested in nothing more than a narcissistic endeavor destined to decimate the lives that you claim to hold dear."

"Go to Hell!" Derrick snarled through gritted teeth as he gathered his strength and shot a wad of blood at his father's face.

Being hit with the gory spitball, Krone reared back with wide, disgusted eyes, instantly unsheathing a blade from inside his jacket pocket. In one quick motion, he thrust it into Derrick and sliced through his side without a moment's hesitation.

Derrick screamed in agony and squeezed his eyes shut as he felt the blade run him through. A cool, sharp hiss was accompanied by a white-hot singe that coursed through his body. It wasn't the first time he was stabbed and he seriously doubted he was lucky enough for it to be his last, but no matter how many times he felt the scorch of a blade, the pain never lessened.

"No!" Lily whaled without outrage at the same time that he retracted the blade.

Instantly, the cool hiss transformed into a dragon's breath of fire, bringing with it a thick river of crimson flowing out of the fresh wound. "What are you doing?" She demanded, breathless and hysterical. "You're going to kill him!"

"Kill him?" His expression darkened into a sadistic quip of ridicule. Again, his eyes glistened as his gaze moved from Derrick, tauntingly towards Lily. He took a moment to settle, letting the ominous words steep in their minds, after proving to them both exactly what he was capable of, before speaking again. "No, I'm afraid you are gravely mistaken. I'm not going to kill him. I'm temporarily crippling him, so that when I kill you, he won't have even the slightest chance of coming to your aid, but don't worry...He'll live."

Hearing the confirmation of his worst fears, Derrick was reanimated and fueled by hate. He knew that he couldn't allow his father to do this. Krone was so smug, so insolent, that Derrick wanted to tear his face off with his bare hands and smash his skull into a million pieces. He wanted to destroy him and his arrogance completely.

He yelled out, propelling all of his weight forward in a manic attempt to break free. He pulled at the ropes, ignoring the sting and using the slickness that was wrought from his own blood to work to his advantage. He heard a crack as he thrashed and hoped that was the post and not his own body breaking. In this moment, his adrenaline was so high, he hardly felt anything. His body was completely numb. The only pain he felt was that of the thought of Krone killing Lily and keeping his daughter from him forever.

He groaned and huffed as he yanked at the ropes until finally, a large, collective snap broke the wood and loosened the binds enough for him to break free.

Wasting no time, Derrick ran towards Lily, standing close, protectively keeping her behind him.

Standing there, between his father and Lily, Derrick felt a pulse thumping against his side in a continual beat. He was certain that with each thrum, more of his blood spilled out, soaking into his shirt and dripping down his side, but he felt no pain. Even the loss of blood wasn't debilitating enough to burst through the fear and torment that he experienced upon the confirmation of his father's intentions.

After all, physical pain was only so debilitating. He had spent a lifetime jeering the thrashes and threats inflicted by his father and the people who worked for him. Yet, the idea that someone he loved, someone completely innocent; his family, nonetheless, was going to be harmed, simply because it would hurt him, was more than Derrick could stomach.

He needed to save Lily and Eva. He couldn't let his father ruin their lives as he had tried to ruin his.

Chapter 9

Gritting his teeth, Derrick narrowed his eyes, taking a pugnacious stance against his father and the men he had brought with him.

"Leave her the fuck alone." Derrick breathed in warning. He heard the sanguinary rattle in his throat and wondered how long his body would be physically able to hold him. Still, he pressed on. "You proved your point. Now, let them go." He growled as his eyes darted suspiciously around the room waiting for someone to make a move that he would need to counter.

If there weren't more of them than he knew he could handle with Lily close enough to be used against him, Derrick wouldn't have thought twice about giving into the urge to kill them.

He still contemplated how he could accomplish their deaths, in order to help Lily escape. Yet, he knew that staying on the defensive, only striking to protect Lily, was his best course of action.

Therefore, he remained still and at the ready as his father voiced a piercing chortle.

"Not only have I proved my point, I have also gotten exactly what I came for. You seem to think that you are valuable to me." His voice was jeering. "When in fact, you were rendered worthless the moment Eric proved to be more gifted than you and now that there is an entirely new generation..." He chuckled. "You and your abilities are a rotary phone in a world saturated by cellular innovation. You are but a footnote in my research, where your daughter, on the other hand, has the potential to headline."

"I have experience. I can help you, far more than a child...a baby ever could. Regardless of her abilities, I am more use to you now."

"Greatness was never achieved by betting on the present. Your baby is an investment; one that should yield a reward that the sum of our talents couldn't possibly compete with."

"What happens if you lose your bet? What happens if the gene isn't passed down?" Derrick demanded, his breath thick with the macabre hindrance of free-flowing blood and bile. "You know that I can help you. You know that I am capable and willing to do what you need me to do...Anything you need me to do."

"No. I am quite certain that you can't." His father insisted a moment before Derrick heard the wind whistle hastily as a tiny fragment exploded out of a contained space. It wasn't loud enough to be a gun, but the projectile was bearing similar speed when whatever was being shot pierced his back.

The sting was unexpected, causing Derrick to reach up to grab whatever stabbed him, giving the man closest to him the opportunity to tackle him to the ground.

Immediately, Derrick knew something was wrong. He knew the man was coming for him and tried to react, but his body simply refused to cooperate. He felt the man tackle him to the ground, as two others aided the first man, rendering Derrick at his knees.

He fought against them as his head was yanked back, forcing him to watch his father's actions. However, his limbs felt heavy and each movement he made caused them to sag more.

Soon, it felt as though he was encased in a straitjacket laced with lead.

Although he remained completely conscious, he was rendered completely, horrifyingly immobile.

Every part of him, including his chest, was crushed by the invisible weight that ensnared him.

The dread of suffocation overtook him.

Throughout his limited conscious thought process, Derrick realized the needle that had burrowed itself into his back must have injected him with a substance that caused this reaction.

Once again, he tried to move, building up his energy for one burst of meaningful power, but to his horror, when he tried to channel the effort, it simply drained from his body without a single muscle complying with his command.

Shit! He thought as the true repercussions of his present situation started to plague him. Derrick tried to ward off the panic that was consuming him, but eventually, the struggle to breathe became all-consuming. His caving chest left him vulnerable and completely unable to retaliate against the men who had overpowered him.

"What did you do to him?" Lily demanded, aghast, as Krone stepped toward her with evil intent.

His eyes glistened with elated ire as his thin lips curled into a sadistic sneer.

"Oh, my dear, if I were you, I would be far more concerned with my own well-being." He cackled, reaching his hand towards her. He grasped a strand of her hair and curled it around his long finger.

Lily recoiled, instantly yanking her head away from him in one quick motion.

"Get away from her!" Derrick growled through gasps of feigning breath.

In his mind, he was thrashing and fighting to free himself, but in reality, his efforts were expelled uselessly.

A flicker of elation coursed through Krone's expression. Inspiration beckoned as his eyes were set ablaze with derision.

He sneered, ensuring that Derrick was forced to endure every inch of his purposeful movements.

Derrick snarled as Krone sauntered closer to Lily. Once he had pivoted behind her, he lightly ran his fingers through her hair, tugging the strands off her shoulder.

His gaze taunted Derrick as he drew his nose up the nape of her neck, towards her ear, sensually inhaling her natural scent, affronting the intimacy that she and Derrick shared.

When Lily tried to pull away, Krone grasped a portion of her hair in his fist and tilted her head back, so that he could hold her flesh against his azure suit.

With his lips close to her ear, he sneered in a malevolent manner.

"You're so beautiful, Lily..." He insisted in a salacious, breathless whisper. "So young and vibrant..." He chuckled. "It's such a shame that you have such...poor choice in the company you keep."

Lily swallowed hard and tried to tug her head away from him, glaring sideways and showing her contempt.

"All of this youthful splendor, going to go to waste for what? For him?" He scoffed in Derrick's direction, yanking her head up farther so that he could force his gaze upon her face.

His eyes were cold and demeaning.

Lily glared back at him, trying not to show her fear.

However, when Krone brought the blade that still gleamed with Derrick's blood up to her face, her bravado wavered.

"Tell me, dear, when you woke up this morning, did you think that you were going to die today?" Krone inquired calmly as he drew the blade down and calmly pressed it against her throat.

Chapter 10

Horrified, Lily drew in a quivering breath, gasping loudly and visibly shaking.

"No!" Derrick screamed, still desperately fighting against the paralysis that plagued him. "Please...No...Kill me!"

"Oh, so now you've resorted to groveling?" His beguiled expression erupted loudly in Lily's ear.

"God dammit, Krone!" He barked in a voice so loud and so desperate that his voice cracked. "Kill me, not her!"

"How magnificently futile..." He mused.

"Yes, I am begging you!" He huffed as he felt as though his lungs were filling with blood and bile, drowning him. "I will beg. I will plead. I will do whatever you want..."

Every few words, Derrick was forced to stop in order to gasp but continued as soon as he was able.

"She's not a threat to you..." He swallowed hard, feeling a thick glob of blood coat his throat. He coughed, which rattled his caving chest, causing him to wheeze.

"And you believe that you are?" He taunted as Lily made an attempt to get to him, but was yanked back, wincing from the threat of the knife as the blade sliced into her throat.

Once she was back, completely under Krone's control, he left the depth of the blade pressing into her neck to remind her the leverage he held.

"I'm not." Derrick insisted, drawing in a loud, painful breath. "I never have been...but if you want to kill someone, fine. Kill me. Torture me. Experiment on me. Do whatever you want to me, but please...let her live..."

"Look at him..." Krone scoffed in a low hiss, forcing Lily close to him through the duress imposed upon her by the blade.

She wriggled uncomfortably, drawing in a shuddering breath. As emotion and fear built up in her throat, she gulped and squeezed her eyes shut.

Tears streamed down her face as she did.

"Look at him!" Krone boomed, pushing her head forward, while the henchmen that held Derrick reared his head up further, forcing him to glare upwards, reaffirming the helplessness that afflicted him. "Such a pathetic waste...of your life, most assuredly. What would possess you to have a child with this man?"

"Please..." She breathed, this time, unable to control her terror.

"What's the matter? You're not so tough when truly facing your own mortality, are you?" He chastised.

"Stop it!" Derrick screamed, causing his voice to become hoarse. Frustrated by his inability to move, he tried to compel his body to battle the paralytic that coursed through his blood, but the only advancement he made was that of his rage.

He snarled at Krone, but his father's eyes only gleamed.

As their gaze connected, Derrick realized, with horror, that he knew the expression that his father wore well.

His eyes grew wide with fright.

"No..." He warned, shaking his head. His heart was thudding loudly in his chest. His ears were ringing and despite his injuries, he was sure that it was the nightmare he found himself in that caused the surreal sensation to overtake him.

The satisfied sneer that marked Krone's features was cunning and evil. It struck terror into his son as he yanked Lily's head back and started to slide the knife deep across her flesh.

A cry of horror rapidly distorted into an appalling gurgle as crimson flowed from the wound, following close behind the constant splitting of her skin.

"No!" Derrick bellowed with such a force that seemed to rattle his entire world before it shattered completely.

Forced to watch, he helplessly witnessed the entirety of her demise.

It didn't take Lily long to know she was dying.

Derrick could see the truth embedded in the depths of her eyes, which were rapidly losing their luster as they transformed from horror to imminent futility.

Pallor consumed her as the crimson washed down the front of her like the wave of a plague.

Still, the instinct to survive consumed her and he listened as her body gasped for breath, despite her awareness that any attempt to persevere would prove to be insufficient.

After three harrowing, unsuccessful pants, even her body decided that death was imminent.

She locked a feeble gaze on Derrick and tried to speak. The garbled words were thick but indecipherable.

"I'm so sorry..." He bellowed, finding that his breath was also nonexistent as the world he knew and loved bled out in front of him.

The words fell from his lips with a hollow uselessness, despite the fact that he could never say enough to truly express his contrition.

After all, he had completely failed her and he knew at that moment that there was nothing that could assuage his guilt.

Once her throat was slit completely, Krone let her go and watched with intense fascination as her limp body crashed to the floor of the warehouse.

Witnessing all of this, with everything going on both inside of his battered body and throughout his tortured mind, he couldn't be sure that this was actually happening.

In his mind, he hoped, prayed and pleaded for all of this to be one terrible trick; a daydream or a hallucination of some sort. He would prefer any form of torment, other than the confirmation of this being the truth.

However, when her body hit the ground with an ominous thud, Derrick had no doubt that this was his new, terrible reality.

"Lily..." He cried, fighting wildly to get to her, to be with her for whatever time she had left.

Unfortunately, the more he struggled the harder it seemed for him to focus.

As he watched Lily's blood pool beneath her lifeless body, Derrick's own blood pumped rapidly in his head, causing him to feel increasingly faint.

Exhaustion engulfed him and eventually, black dots, like morbid fireworks, exploded in his vision. His mind felt as though it was pummeled with sandbags, weighing heavily atop his brain, making it impossible for him to think.

The ringing in his ears grew louder as his manic screams of disbelief faded into the background, he felt the darkness ensnare him.

He battled the nothingness that hastily devoured him with every fiber of his remaining fortitude, but in the end, the blackness swallowed him whole.

Chapter 11

In a panic, Derrick's eyes snapped opened.

"Lily!" He screamed as he tried to sit up, only to be thwarted by a sharp, piercing pain that cascaded through his entire body, forcing all of the air from his lungs.

He gasped, momentarily overcome by his panic before ceasing all attempts at movement abruptly.

Realizing that trying to move wasn't in his best interest, if even possible, he decided to take stock of his injuries and surroundings before trying to move again. He groaned, gasping a painful breath. Blood still coated his tongue and caused a sticky, coagulated crust to further impair the small amount of movement he was capable of.

He felt carpet, matted and likely saturated beneath him. He chanced another attempt at movement, shoving himself over, onto his back with one hasty push. His body revolted and he screamed in agony as the skin where his side was split open severed again, instantly seeping out a fresh gush of gore, adding to the already coagulated flood of crimson.

The light pierced his eyes, racking his skull and causing his headache to worsen.

Eventually, though, after enduring a few more agonizing breaths, he was able to chance another attempt to survey his surroundings. As he feared, the sudden burst of light caused his head to feel as though it was being blown apart in slow motion, while his muscles ached in protest as he raised his arm to shield his sight.

When his eyes adjusted to the brightness, Derrick realized that he was back in Eva's room.

After staring up at the ceiling for a time, attempting to regain his composure, Derrick readied himself for the burst of anguish he would experience the moment he moved.

He drew in a few more cautious breaths and rolled over, completely ignoring the uproar from his body.

He looked around.

Despite the blood, which he assumed was his own and the shattered tablet, which lay only a few feet away from him, everything seemed to be exactly the way he left it.

His whole world was ripped from his grasp with only his wracked body, a pool of blood and a broken piece of technology to prove that it had happened.

His heart ached and he felt sick.

However, his physical afflictions were nothing compared to the emotional train wreck he felt repeatedly colliding inside of him each time he thought about what had happened to Lily and what still might be happening to Eva.

Haunted by this knowledge, Derrick wanted to die.

Yet, despite his need to end the pain that tortured him, he knew that he couldn't act on that instinct because his daughter was still in danger.

His last remaining hope for some kind of peace was that he could still save her and if he did, she would need him now, more than ever. Thus, he couldn't die. He needed to endure whatever was necessary and a confidence that he would bring Eva home.

I have to find her! He thought, forcing himself to stand. He ignored the scream of rippling pain and cracking bones that threatened to render him unconscious until he was completely upright.

However, with one misstep, the pressure he placed on his injured leg proved to be too much and it buckled beneath him.

Inadvertently, he yelled out as he crashed to the ground.

Breathing heavily and wheezing within every exhale, Derrick groaned.

The discomfort that now breached the entirety of his existence in waves of nausea as his broken body shook, disabled him completely. He moaned and closed his eyes, unable to take the constant spinning that he encountered each time he attempted to open his eyes.

"Derrick?" He heard a familiar voice call from down the hall.

Instantly, panic struck him.

Although he didn't fear the voice, the idea that someone could be lying in wait for his brother, using his inability to defend himself as bait caused his stomach to lurch. He clenched his teeth together tightly and inhaled deeply, even though the motion hurt, simply to keep from throwing up.

He couldn't bear the sight of another person he loved getting hurt because of his own weakness.

"Go away!" Derrick bellowed, hoping that Eric wasn't dumb enough to disregard his command.

Yet, he should have known better.

When his voice reached Eric, his footsteps hastened.

Eric rushed into the room but stopped short at the sight of Derrick laying on the ground.

"Oh my God!" He hissed, aghast at the sight, sinking to his knees next to him.

Eric moved to touch his shoulder but thought better of it.

"What the hell happened?" He demanded.

When Derrick gazed up at Eric, he saw that the color was rapidly receding from his face. His expression was grim.

"I'm fine." He grumbled. "You need to leave."

"No!" He insisted, his eyes searched over his body, taking stock of his injuries. His voice shook with concern as he continued. "You need a hospital..."

"No. No hospital. No doctor. I don't need the attention." He winced as he tried to

100

sit up, but stopped when he found that he was currently physically unable.

"What's going on?" Eric demanded, now growing agitated. Glancing around the room, however, his voice lowered and fear struck it as he shuddered. "Please tell me that Lily and Eva..."

The distressed, daunting glower that Derrick shot him caused Eric to refrain from finishing his comment.

"My God..." He breathed. "What happened? Are they okay? Where are they?"

"No," Derrick answered with a hint of warning ringing throughout his voice.

"No?" Eric demanded, his voice thick with concern. "No, what?"

Swallowing hard, his eyes bore deeply into his brother's gaze. His expression was grim and emotions caused his already exasperated voice to falter as he tried to speak.

"You asked if they were okay..." He hissed, unable to bring himself to say the words. "I answered you."

He grumbled and compelled himself to sit up, sure that he would rather endure the pain of walking away from Eric than that of putting the atrocities of his own stupidity into words.

Eric's jaw hinged open with shock. His eyes darkened with pity and confusion. When he spoke again, his voice was shaken and withered; quiet.

"Der...You don't mean..." He drew in a fearful breath and let it out hastily. "Where are they?"

"Lily's dead!" Derrick screamed, whipping around to face Eric again, besetment poisoning his dangerous tone.

Stunned, Eric shrank back.

"No...There's got to be some mistake..." His words fell thoughtlessly and frantically out of his mouth.

"There's no goddamn mistake, Eric! I watched her die!" Derrick's voice boomed, cracking with fervent wrath and vile potency.

"Wait, what?" Eric's voice now faltered. He stood up, reaching out, presumably to try to comfort his older brother, but Derrick didn't want any of it.

Since she died because he loved her, he didn't want anyone's condolences or pity. It only added to his guilt.

His singular ambition was to get Eva back. Afterward, he would do everything in his power to ensure that his father paid for what he did to Lily.

Presently, though, he only had one objective and mourning was not conducive to the only remaining reason that he was still alive.

"Don't touch me!" Derrick hissed, drawing himself away from his brother, using the bed, instead for leverage. "Krone destroyed my family. He took Eva

and...Lily's gone." He couldn't bring himself to admit the truth again, now that his fury had returned to a slow simmer instead of a vexed eruption of emotion.

"I can help you...Please..." Eric insisted,

not the least bit afraid of Derrick's volatile state. He inched towards him, closing the gap between them.

"No." Derrick insisted backing up and

glowering at him with a warning. "I don't need you to help yourself right into a trap. I need to find my daughter by myself and if I die saving her, I need to know that you'll be able to raise her...keep

her safe."

"Of course, but..." Eric winced as though he was about to say something that he knew would hurt him.

"But what?" He demanded as his legs started to shake and his eyes became slightly unfocused.

"You can't go after Eva...Not right now. Not like this. You wouldn't stand a chance against him."

"I heal fast. I'll be ready for the bastard by the time I find him." He insisted propelling himself forward.

Eric stopped him.

"Sure, you heal fast. We both do," He insisted, attempting to reason with him. "But do you realize that if you didn't your injuries would probably keep you comatose...if they didn't kill you?"

"Yeah, well they didn't and I'm still alive, so there is nothing in the world that is going to keep me from finding my daughter." He tried to push past him but lost his balance putting forth the effort and staggered forward.

Eric caught him and helped him back up, shooting him a meaningful expression.

"No 'I told you so' shit," Derrick grumbled as Eric helped him out into the living room and onto the couch.

"I wasn't going to say a word." He insisted, his eyes resting on him with commiseration.

Derrick despised it.

"You don't deserve that." He added with an understanding tone. "I can't imagine...how you must feel, or what you must be going through but you can barely stand." He narrowed his eyes. "How are you going to do anything more than amuse Krone in your current state?"

Derrick shot him a look of warning, but knowing that Eric was right, he chose to take his point rather than the blatant insensitivity of his comment.

"I'm sorry..." He replied, almost immediately, genuinely apologetic.

Derrick's shoulders rose and fell in an uncaring fashion and his gaze wavered from his brother's lazily distancing himself from a reality that he still couldn't quite bring himself to believe.

It occurred to him at that moment that there was no way he would be able to stay here.

Considering that Lily was the primary decorator virtually everything that surrounded him came from her. She picked out the couch that he was sitting on the coffee table in front of him and the paint that glared back at him from the walls.

In doing this she had always managed to make the house feel like home.

Until today this was the place that Derrick had always wanted to be. It was the first true home he had ever had but today that too was ruined by his father's wrath.

As his mind wandered into a dark solitary place he found that the walls that were once the brick and mortar of his happy home now taunted him. The pictures that were strewn about in gloriously normal fashion were now nothing more than cruel beaming jeers; memories from the life that he was suddenly pointlessly severed from.

He felt himself swallow hard as the eyes in the pictures and the memories of how furniture and trinkets came to be assaulted him encouraging his guilt.

His gaze couldn't escape the reminders of his failure.

He had built a life with Lily here; welcomed their daughter and planned their future within these walls. Now she was dead and their daughter was missing.

Eva's fate remained undecided for the moment but regardless of his efforts, their lives would never be the same again.

He knew in that moment without a doubt that he couldn't possibly stay here.

Once he retrieved Eva he would have to move not only for her safety but for the preservation of his sanity.

Chapter 12

It didn't take long for Eric to notice that Derrick had ventured into his own mind and tried his best to bring him back to reality as quick as possibly.

Unfortunately, the reality wasn't any better than the deepest, darkest crevices of Derrick's warped mind.

"Derrick? Derrick!" He heard Eric exclaim in a worried fashion only a moment before he felt his hand on his shoulder.

Shaking himself out of his morbid thoughts he turned his attention towards Eric.

"What?" He hissed his eyes glaring dangerously. He wasn't particularly upset over being torn from his daunting thoughts but the situation he found himself in caused him to be volatile.

"I'm worried about you..." Eric stated his voice sounding almost as aberrant as Derrick felt.

"Yeah well don't be." He grumbled. "I'm certainly not fine but I have my purpose."

"Hey, what's that?" Eric asked as his eyes flickered up in an inquisitive fashion, motioning towards the computer monitor that sat on the desk on the other side of the room.

Instantly, Derrick's heart leaped with ire. His eyes were ablaze with concern. His tension mounted as he turned around, before Eric could instruct him otherwise.

Seeing another taunting note, with the same written provocation as the one that had officially started this nightmare, a terrible fury combusted inside of him. He clenched his teeth and growled with contempt.

Ignoring the fresh angst that rose up inside of him the moment that he got to his feet, he staggered over to the computer.

Knowing he couldn't stop him, Eric simply tried to offer his assistance, but Derrick shoved past him; far more concerned with his rage than with giving into the injuries he sustained.

He hobbled over to the desktop and yanked the message off the screen.

Crumpling it in his hand, he tossed it aside.

With his good hand, he swatted the mouse to wake the machine and waited to see what was in store for him. As soon as the screen flickered to life, Derrick was forced into a sick and twisted sense of déjà vu, except instead of Lily, it was Eva who filled the still image.

She didn't look distressed, fortunately. In fact, she appeared to be playing. Her back was to the camera, though, so Derrick couldn't be sure, but it appeared as though she had no idea she was being filmed.

Still, the innocence of the opening image didn't boast much confidence. While he was glad to see that she didn't appear to have any idea what was going on and didn't seem to feel threatened, she was still very much in danger and that terrified him.

Wondering what Krone would force him to endure now, through this video, Derrick felt his knees buckle, but the weakness had nothing to do with his physical afflictions.

It was all he could do to stagger into the chair.

"What?" Eric demanded, seeing his older brother's sudden enhanced distress. He rushed over to the computer and followed his eyes to the screen. "Oh..." He replied, surmising the fear that Derrick had and sounding intensely sympathetic.

The two were quiet for a long moment. The hum of the desktop and the creaks of the house were the only audible exceptions in an otherwise silent house.

"Ummm..." Eric started cautiously. "Would...Would you like me to watch it for you?"

"No." He hissed as shock and trepidation were suddenly replaced by intense anger. He drew in an ireful breath and huffed it back out, glaring at the screen. He reached out his hand and clasped it tightly around the mouse, almost as though he intended to take his frustrations out on it.

"You know; you don't have to do this right now." Eric insisted with an understanding tone.

"If it'll help me find my daughter..." He took a deep, calming breath before issuing a curt nod. "I have to know."

Before he wasted another moment on the contemplation of the unknown, Derrick clicked the play button and hoped to God this video would prove to be more helpful than hurtful.

He wasn't sure how much abuse he could take before completely losing his mind for good.

As the video loaded, Derrick's heart started to pound, but when it started to play, he couldn't help but feel a wad of emotion build up in the back of his throat.

He realized now that the slightly distorted video, made from the webcam on the old laptop was created in this very room.

Eva was here? He thought, loathing the idea that she was so close, probably while he lay unconscious in the other room and he had failed to save her. He hadn't even known she was there. Yet, considering the state he was in at the time, it was probably best that she was oblivious. He didn't want her to see him like this and he couldn't stand the thought of her getting hurt, due to his ineptitude.

Eva walked around the house in a confident fashion like she had since the day she learned it was easier to move herself than have someone move her.

She bopped around the house with a strange sense of ease.

It was almost as though she was looking for something.

Eva seemed to be cooperative and didn't say anything to the people in the room with her. Instead, she made a point of stopping to stare out the window and glance down the hall.

Eventually, he realized that what he first thought was ease, was actually caution. He had seen that look before when she was obviously trying to get away with something. She was overly accommodating and had a knack for knowing what was expected of her, but when no one was looking, she would do what she wanted.

He realized that she was doing this now. Every once and awhile, she would turn back towards the camera as though checking to see if she was being watched before inching towards the hallway.

Derrick felt his jaw tighten with morbid anticipation.

Unfortunately, when she got too close to the hallway, which was what led to her room, where he was now positive he was stashed during the filming of this video, he watched as one of the henchmen lead Eva out of the room, towards the kitchen.

He watched her glare at the man, but before he noticed, she returned to her overly-agreeable nature.

Once she was out of sight, Krone positioned himself in front of the camera.

He sat down in the very seat that Derrick was seated in now. His leer was taunting.

Derrick's anxiety heightened, his eyes glued to the screen.

In the silence that followed, he wondered if he should've taken Eric up on his offer to watch the video for him, but quickly shoved the thought from his mind.

This was between him and Krone. If anyone was going to stumble upon the key to getting his daughter back, it would be him. Thus, he continued to stare, hoping that he could endure whatever came next.

Chapter 13

Immediately, Krone's eyebrows raised and his expression mocked the emotion he knew his son would be feeling when he saw this video. Yet, it was a near certainty that while he comprehended the emotion that a father should have, he had probably never felt an ounce of it for himself.

"She might look well adjusted, Derrick, but she continues to ask where her Mommy and Daddy are..." Krone insisted in a low voice.

Trying to keep his composure, Derrick drew in a deep breath, growled and narrowed his eyes as his heart sank.

"She seems particularly curious as to why you haven't come to her aid." He went on, propelling a deep-throated chuckle. "I suppose her mother instilled the same, obviously false, sense of security in her daughter." His eyes leered. "The inaccurate assurance that Daddy was always going to be there to save her."

Rage washed over him. His jaw locked as he bore his teeth. He inhaled a shallow breath in an equally useless attempt to distance himself from the agony brought on by Krone's baiting.

"Der..." He heard Eric behind him, watching his brother tense. His eyes remained fixed on the computer screen.

He ignored him, barely even hearing his words over the boiling manifestation of rage, which tore opened his all-too-fresh wounds. His body shook with rage as his eyes connected with the man's on the screen, wishing he could go through it and rip the bastard's throat out.

"Of course, you'll never find her." Krone insisted, as though the two of them were carrying on a conversation in person.

"Okay..." Eric chimed in, louder this time, reaching for the mouse to pause the video, but Derrick shoved his hand aside.

"No!" He hissed menacingly, shooting a glare of warning behind him. "Leave it."

"This isn't good for you...He isn't going to tell you anything useful...."

"Shut up!" He bellowed only a moment before Krone started to speak again.

"After she leaves this house, with me, it will be the last time she sees anything familiar to her. Don't worry, though. She isn't completely apprised of everything that has gone on today. Instead, every time she asks about you, I remind her that. Sadly, Mommy and Daddy don't want her anymore. They aren't looking for her. They gave her up...That's why she's here."

Derrick drew in a hasty breath as Krone paused. His eyes were aflame with animosity and tremors coursed through his body.

As though knowing that Derrick would have a similar reaction, he rebuked his actions with the gleaming of his piercing eyes, while his lips tugged upwards with scornful, fiendish pleasure.

"I imagine that you wouldn't have approved of me explaining the gory details that encompass the truth. Certainly, you aren't so that you would rather your daughter be terrified, knowing that she is ultimately going to endure the same fate as her mother, all so that she knows the pathetic truth? That her father failed to rescue her...as well as her mother and that his petty attempts to retrieve her are only prolonging the inevitable realization that I have won?"

Yearning to contain the ravenous urge of vengeance that boiled his blood, Derrick moved to stand up, with every intention of attacking the screen that sat before him. Although he knew that he wouldn't be harming the face of the man who filled his reality with his worst nightmares, the need for violence consumed him.

"Stop it!" Eric yelled, immediately grabbing his shoulder and forcing him back down, into his seat.

In his weakened state, there was nothing he could do to fight him. Thus, he simply drew in a deep breath and relied on every bit of stamina he had to keep from lashing out at the inanimate object.

This time, Eric did take the opportunity of Derrick's distraction to pause the video.

Instead of Krone's face, Eric promptly filled his brother's vision. He looked angry, his face red with rage and teetering on emotion, but Derrick didn't care about how he was feeling. He wanted a clue. He wanted to know what he had to say.

"What are you doing? Turn it back on!" He demanded, trying to push past him.

Eric didn't budge.

"This is stupid. He isn't going to tell you anything useful and all you're doing is torturing yourself." His brow furrowed with concern and his eyes softened. "You've been through enough. You don't need this. He's only going to hurt you."

"He might not mean to, but there could be something in this stupid video that helps me find my daughter." Without meaning to, he gazed up with a certain vulnerability that he loathed.

He wished he didn't feel anything. If he hadn't, he wouldn't have this problem and even if he did, he wouldn't be clouded by sentiment.

Instead, he could find his daughter and bring her home.

He couldn't help but think, if he wasn't so consumed by the genuine feelings he had for his family, he might have been able to save her.

Yet, he knew he couldn't go there.

His mind was already in a bad enough place. Opening that realm of possibilities would surely be the final blow to his already waning mental stability.

The expression that Eric returned with only caused him to hate his reaction more.

"I'm here to help you."

Derrick's moment of weakness swiftly morphed into genuine exasperation.

"Well, then fucking help me!" He screamed, causing Eric to narrow his eyes. "Treating me like a child, like I can't handle this, isn't doing anything but wasting time."

"Derrick, watching this video is wasting time!" He retorted, crossing his arms across his chest in a confrontational manner. "And by the way, I know for a fact that you can't handle this. If you could, you'd be as bad as Krone. No one in their right mind could *handle* this, so stop being an asshole and let me help you."

At first, he opened his mouth to retort, his anger flowing viciously towards his brother, but thought better of it. Instead, he simply narrowed his eyes and spoke with a warning.

"Get out of the way. I want to at least watch it to the end..." He huffed a sigh and forced himself to sound like he had regained some composure, even though he knew that he hadn't. "Please."

Eric didn't move at first. He stood in front of the computer, stubbornly glaring at his older brother. Discretion and discernment weighed heavily in his gaze.

Finally, though, he stepped aside and Derrick continued to play the video.

As though realizing his thought process, without even being aware that he was watching it, Krone shook his head, almost as though he was disappointed. A low, cocky chuckle erupted from deep within Krone's throat before he continued to prod him.

"Yet, salvaging your pride was the farthest thing from my mind in telling your daughter that you abandoned her. My true motivation was to instill an early seed of hatred." He beamed. "When forging a potential weapon, it is best to fuel the ammunition with the most potent toxin one can muster."

"What the hell does that mean?" Eric demanded, his attention now returned fully to the screen.

"Shh!" Derrick hissed.

"Of course, she doesn't believe me...At least not yet." He snickered. "But as time wears on, I have a feeling she will come to appreciate my version of events as a plausible possibility." His shoulders rose and fell with a nonchalant disposition before he added. "Who knows, she might even learn to accept what I tell her as absolute truth. In any case, this will likely be the last view you ever have of your darling daughter...so take a good, hard look."

At this, Krone eased himself out of the way, causing the camera to focus on Eva as she waddled back into the room.

After a moment, the voice of their father came over the footage, low and menacing, as though he was speaking over their shoulder.

"Remember her as she was, Derrick, because I highly doubt that you will like what she is to become."

Chapter 14

Dammit! I knew he shouldn't have watched that... Eric thought as the video ended.

He wanted to measure Derrick's current mental state. Yet, as the screen went black and the whole computer fizzled into nothing more than a heap of metal and crossed wires, he knew it was best not to move.

The empty monitor stared back at the two of them, mirroring reality, complete with the dark cloud that they felt hanging over them, constantly growing, feeding on their grief.

Feeling angry, helpless and confused, Eric stayed quiet and watched his brother digest everything he had insisted on seeing.

He wanted to ask if he was alright, but he knew that would either be insulting, or Derrick would lie to spare his feelings.

Either way, the comment wouldn't be comforting.

Eric knew that there wasn't much at all he could do to make this situation any better. He could only do so much to help find Eva and he certainly couldn't bring Lily back. Thus, he felt useless.

All the abilities I could have and mine is nothing more than self-serving... He thought, automatically feeling bad, on principle for thinking of himself at a time like this.

However, it wasn't only himself, or his abilities, or even the situation as a whole that he was contemplating. He thought about all of it in rapid succession.

He felt his mind sorting through facts and situations, trying to figure out if there was indeed anything that he could do to help.

Unfortunately, he came up empty trying make every rapid thought relevant.

"Well...They couldn't have gotten far." Eric finally decided to say aloud.

"Oh yeah?" Derrick rebuked. "How do you figure? He could've hopped on one of his private planes, gotten halfway across the world by now."

"I don't know about that. I don't think he would go halfway across the world."

Derrick's eyes raised towards his brother with heavy insinuation.

Eric couldn't help but feel slightly taken aback by the expression, but he let it pass. He had a feeling he would have to let a lot slip away without mention. Considering he was going through, far too much for one person to handle, a few suspicious looks were hardly cause to feel insulted.

"Okay, then tell me...Where is he?"

"I don't know." He admitted, ignoring the disappointed scowl that was present on Derrick's face. "But something tells me, that even with a private jet which you seem to think he has, it is much easier to take a kidnapped child across the country, rather than to a different one."

"Not necessarily...I'm sure there's plenty of non-extradition countries that wouldn't think twice about allowing a man like Krone to fly into their airspace and spend money in their country no matter what he did." With a shake of his head, it seemed that his mind cleared a little bit.

Eric wasn't quite sure what that meant, but he couldn't help but think that the calm, focused tone of voice that followed wasn't as encouraging a sign as he would like to believe.

"But, you're right. He's had to be somewhere for the past decade. Hopefully, if we find out what he's been up to, we can find out where he lives."

"Okay..." Eric replied, more concerned with Derrick's mental state than with the subject of the conversation. "But even if you find it, what are you going to do? Barge in there, guns blazing? You can barely stand."

After stating what Eric thought was fairly obvious, he immediately became concerned by the way his brother's eyes hardened and his jaw tightened.

However, he never got the chance to voice his answer. The phone rang and it immediately zapped his attention away from the conversation at hand.

He stared at the number, intently for a moment, his eyes narrowing with wonderment and aggravation.

The number was local, but it wasn't named in his contacts.

After deliberating whether or not to answer it, Derrick scooped up the phone.

"Hello?" His voice was already confrontational, but he listened to what they had to say. "Yes, that's me."

Eric tried to listen in, but despite his best eavesdropping efforts, he couldn't make out who was on the other side of the conversation.

"Is that so?" He inquired, his voice now more unintentionally vulnerable than Eric figured he wanted to be. Still, he kept an even tone as he continued. "No. She told me that her and our daughter were going to spend the week at her mother's house...I'll come down and tell you what I know...Whenever you want. Yeah...Sure."

He hung up the phone but didn't volunteer any information.

Eric waited patiently, but when he simply stared down at the phone, he decided he was going to have to ask him what happened.

"Who was that?"

"That was the police...Apparently, there was a call about a disturbance yesterday. A neighbor who only recently decided to come forward." He rolled his eyes and huffed an angry breath.

"Why do you say it like that? That's great! Maybe they saw something that will help..." Halfway through his encouragement, however, the potent expression that Eric was receiving fizzled the remainder of his comment. "What?"

"It wasn't a neighbor."

"Wait a minute...Why did you lie?" Eric felt his heart start to pound as he seriously contemplated exactly what could be going on in his brother's head.

"Because I can't tell them the truth." He insisted.

"Why? Call them back. Tell them what happened...Show them what happened."

"There's no point!" He insisted. "If I waiver from the plan Krone has concocted, he might..."

Stopping short, Eric was sure that he couldn't bear to finish the thought.

"It's too dangerous. I'll endure whatever I have to, but ultimately, I have to handle this myself."

"They can help you." Eric insisted.

Derrick shook his head with conviction. His eyes were scary and when he spoke, his voice was low, desperate.

"No. They can't. No one can."

"I think you're making a mistake."

"I don't care what you think." He insisted, but his eyes immediately turned to persuasion immediately after his fierce comment. "What I do care about, though, is that you back me up. If anyone asks, you give the same story I did. Be vague, like it was just a passing conversation...something she did frequently."

It was obvious that the concern he was feeling was present on his face. He didn't want to go that route and didn't understand why the truth would be bad.

"Please, Eric...You wanted to know how you could help..." His head bobbed in the direction of the phone. "This is how."

Eric didn't like this idea in the least, but the desperation on Derrick's face reminded him that he knew their father far better than he did. If anyone was going to decipher the best way to deal with Dr. Alexander Krone, he would be the best person for the job.

After all, he did survive Krone's wrath for eight years before he disappeared.

He was willing to bet that was longer than anyone else had.

"Alright..." Eric huffed. "I don't like the idea, but I trust you."

"Thank you."

"Yeah...Sure." He answered, but couldn't completely force himself to mean it.

He was sure that Derrick knew this, but since he didn't question him further, Eric took it as a win and hoped to God he had a plan that wouldn't get him killed.

Chapter 15

The week dragged on with a long, harrowing, relentless, torturous stride.

Every minute felt like hours and days seemed to last an eternity.

Although Derrick noticed an improvement in his physical condition, every second he was forced to be away from his daughter dragged him deeper into a terrorizing catacomb of insanity. He needed to find Eva but knew that he was in no physical condition to attempt a rescue attempt.

The truth was, he didn't even know where to start.

Thus, he was confined to the same house that now tormented him with the memories that were found within.

The police had more questions for him. He was as cooperative as he knew he could be, but he still knew he was their main suspect. They never came out and said it, but they didn't have to.

Krone had made sure that he appeared to be a perfectly packaged psychopath, ripe for the picking.

Perhaps they knew that, though, because after three visits to the police station, telling the same story; that he was mugged while his Lily was, supposedly visiting her mother, they hadn't made an arrest.

Nevertheless, towards the end of the week, he found himself in his mother's house, standing across from her.

They were having an extremely pointed conversation that Derrick didn't want, nor need.

Yet, since he knew that when it came to either of his parents, it was better to know what they wanted than to guess, he endured the torment.

"What are you saying?" Derrick's hazel eyes darkened as he peered at his mother with a flash of contempt.

"Well..." Karen's voice was reserved, cautious as though she was afraid of something.

Afraid of me? Derrick thought but shoved the notion from his mind as he crossed his arms and narrowed his eyes.

Throughout the silence that followed, his shifted weight creaked the floorboards.

In the distance, the washing machine and dryer barreled with a certain constant tempo and birds chirped loudly outside the window behind the object of his harrowed gaze.

"You don't think I had anything to do with this, do you?" He paused. The absurdity of it all almost made him laugh, but the inclination to do so was greatly overshadowed by the wrench of horror that he felt in the pit of his stomach. "You do, don't you?" He accused, his voice husky with emotion. His arms fell from his chest as he stepped towards his mother in askance.

"I don't know what to think!" She exclaimed as tears played at her eyes, causing the crows feet that Karen took great care in otherwise effacing to become visible. Her expression settled on him hard.

"You should believe me!" Derrick bellowed.

He should be aghast at the insinuation that his mother was making, but deep down, he couldn't help but believe that this was typical of her.

"I'm trying, but you don't make it all that easy!"

"I don't know how much easier I can make it for you, mother..." He paused, glaring at her as though to remind her of where her loyalties should lie, but didn't hinge on it. Karen had always put a fat bank account and a good lay ahead of her sons' wellbeing. "I'm telling you the truth. I love my family."

Karen's lips parted with outrage as she realized a hidden meaning within his words. Frustrated, she threw her arms out and bowed slightly, before jutting a hip, full of attitude towards the counter as she crossed her arms.

"How dare you." She spat, her heavily shadowed eyelids tapering.

"Don't be petty." Derrick hissed as he realized how she had taken the comment. He gritted his teeth for a moment, reigning in the anger that she had always brought forth in him.

Karen seemed so oblivious, or otherwise occupied that she had never let on that she knew anything about what her husband was up to.

Growing up, the revelation had always bothered Derrick. She might not have gotten her hands dirty, but he was certain that his mother had looked the other way on more than one occasion when it came to the dealings of his father.

"Then again, do whatever the hell you want!" He grumbled, throwing his hands up in the air and pivoting towards the dining room table that hadn't been used for a formal, family dinner in years.

"Don't you dare walk away from me!" She accosted. Immediately, he heard the click of her heels against the hardwood floor, as she crossed the narrow kitchen and grabbed ahold of his elbow. "I'm not done."

Derrick tensed, but he didn't take another step towards the door.

"Well, I am." He spat, but still didn't move.

"Derrick..." Her voice suddenly faint, as her shoes clicked again, now backward, while her hand lowered away from him.

"What?" His jawline taut as he turned back to face her. She was manipulating him. He knew it and she knew it, but that didn't mean that he wasn't going to let her. When her eyes gazed up at him, filled with enough tears to cause her makeup to run grotesquely, he felt his shoulders relax as he let out a sigh. "What is it?" His voice was softer now, minimally more understanding.

Looking at her now, he was reminded of how much he wanted to hate his mother. God knows, he had enough reasons to. Insinuating that he had betrayed his family, hurt them in any way, was only the most recent in a long trail of unfounded accusations that stretched back to his childhood. However, as much as he wanted to, especially at this moment, turn his back on Karen and leave her to her own warped reality, he couldn't. As terrible as she was, she was still his mother and for whatever reason, that still meant enough to him that he couldn't just walk away.

Her bottom lip tugged inward, her dark, pensive eyes wide, he was sure that he wasn't going to like what she was going to say next.

"I'm moving to California with your father. Eric is coming with me."

Chapter 16

Rage washed through him. His eyes grew hard, focusing on her, trying to decipher exactly what she had said. He knew that she wasn't about to tell him good news, but this was ridiculous. He felt his mouth hinge open as he gaped at her.

"You're going to do what?" He demanded, trying not to show that all of the air was forced from his lungs.

Standing up tall, having told him the brunt of the news, she sucked back her tears and the emotion she had used to get him to listen to her long enough for her to drop the bomb on him and inched back. Her head shot up, her deep rouge lips pursed tightly. Her jaw tightened and her eyes pierced into his, unrelenting and impenitent.

"We're leaving. Tonight."

"To get away from me?" He surmised thickly, backing up until his shoulder blades braced against the wall.

"It isn't like you're the best role model for your brother right now." Karen insisted, but when her son didn't respond, save for a piercing, betrayed scowl marring his features as he realized she was serious, her voice lowered an octave. However, instead of being repentant, she was cross, giving off an air that told him she thought he should be grateful that she was saving his brother from his diabolical clutches.

"You know, Derrick, you went and bought a house at eighteen, got engaged and had a baby...You thought you had your life all figured out, but now, three years later, I have the police coming to my house and interrogating my own family, because of you."

Derrick felt his spine prickle with resentment as his eyes gleamed with fury. The hair on the back of his neck stood on end while his fists clenched. Drawing in a deep breath, he forced the images of what happened to his fiancée and the horrors of what could be happening to his daughter out of his mind. That was the last thing he needed right now.

"I didn't do anything wrong." He asserted, trying to keep his voice from cracking through his rage. "I would never hurt them. I love them."

Them. That was what they were reduced to, if only because Derrick couldn't utter their names without losing control.

"The police..." His mother started, nervously. Her heels clicked again as she took a few steps towards him.

"To hell with the police!" Derrick snarled, his ears ringing as his blood pressure rose. "You shouldn't be concerned with what the police think. You should only care about finding the woman I love and your granddaughter. Leaving the state should be the last thing on your mind!"

"You say you're trying to protect your family..." She hissed, hurtfully as another few taps of her shoes brought her close enough so that she could poke a hard finger into Derrick's shoulder. "Well, I'm trying to protect my family. Between the questions that the police were asking me about the disappearances and all of your secrets, I feel I'm justified to do whatever I need to in order to feel safe."

"From me?" He breathed, his eyes settling, defeated on his mother as he backed up until the corner of the wall dug into his back. He shifted his weight as the house whined again, as his desperate tone lingered in the air, souring more with every moment that passed.

Gazing into Karen's eyes, seeing the genuine fear cloud her judgment; a fear that her husband had clearly instilled, he wanted to tell his mother what had really happened. There was a part of him that yearned to express what he had seen and why, despite everything that had transpired between the two of them, his stomach tightened uncomfortably at the thought of her going back with her husband.

However, she had never believed him before. Time and time again, he was betrayed by her.

Which was why, this time, he didn't even try.

Although, he'd be damned if he let her take his brother away from him. He certainly couldn't let her force Eric into the clutches of the man who had singlehandedly ruined his life.

He felt his teeth mash together so hard, his gums ached. A growl erupted from his throat as he pressed away from the wall. Although he felt the sting of rage singing him more with every second that passed, encapsulated by his mother's hard stance, he tried to appeal to her.

"Let Eric stay here. You can do whatever you want, but I don't think that California is the best place for him." He was trying to stay calm, approachable, diplomatic and agreeable. His arms shifted to cross over his chest, but he thought better of it. He didn't want to give his mother any more of a reason to doubt his intentions.

Closing himself off would be his undoing. He was sure of it.

"No." She breathed. "As much as you like to think that he is your responsibility, Eric is my son...Your father and I think..."

Rage rippled through him at the mention of his father. How dare she try to create such a false sense of family at a time like this. Usually, he didn't care what his mother spewed about her husband and the relationship that was wrought by him and his children, but today, the words cut too deep.

Knowing the truth and being unable to express it, to anyone without putting his daughter at more of a risk, burned through the depths of his soul causing him to become crazed with vexation.

"I don't care what he says!" Derrick screamed, unable to bridle in his anger any further. He stepped towards his mother as his eyebrows drew in and his fists clenched. His breath was heightened with his exasperation.

Karen backed up, her heels clacking hastily until her backside hit the cabinets. Immediately, her hands spread out behind her as her nails danced across the counter.

Since he hadn't moved, only raised his voice, Derrick knew that her alarm was only to show he had played right into the reaction she wanted from him. His small retaliation had only justified her actions; at least in her own mind.

"Come now, Derrick...Don't make this more difficult than it already is." A familiar, wretched voice, which teetered on the brink of an English accent caused his abrupt shift in focus. The scent of burnt cherries wafted lazily into the room before the puffing of the pipe and the man who drew it in.

Long, thin fingers coiled around the ornate, ivory stem, a stark contrast to the Cherrywood bowl that sloped down off of the bit that fit squarely between his thin lips. It was obvious that the old man was aging; his hair cut close, had whitened to match the tightly shaven beard and mustache he had worn for years.

However, his sickening stride and unwavering confidence, boasted by his dignified persona never changed. His azure suit was finely pressed and immaculate, despite the blood that was shed to buy it and his crisp, clean shirt fit his thin frame with precision. Accents of crimson on his perfectly astute Eldredge Tie Knot and the matching handkerchief whispered of his true intentions, while the sterling silver, dagger tie-clip gored at the heart of his guise.

However, no one, not even his wife seemed to either be able or want to look past his stable façade.

Deep-set, hazel eyes glared at Derrick with a warning, while his russet wing tipped shoe clacked against the kitchen floor, preceded only by his ebony cane, which illuminated his presence with the coruscating diamond mounted on the claws of a lustrous silver collar.

Hate engulfed his son. Burning, consuming malice washed over him as memories of what this man had done to those that he loved culminated rapidly in his mind.

At the sight of the man, Derrick could no longer restrain himself.

In that moment of crazed ineptitude, he didn't care who was watching, or what the repercussions might be.

His solitary thought was to make Krone bleed.

Derrick knew that he could be violent and ruthless if he wanted to be. After all, he was his father's son and now that the chance was practically gift-wrapped, he would allow Krone to experience, firsthand what his influence had wrought.

His only hope at that moment was that the old man's heart didn't give out before Derrick was finished.

Reflexively, Derrick's eyes searched his immediate surroundings for a weapon. His hand thrust out and his fingers coiled around the first object he found that seemed satisfactory; appropriate even.

As he unsheathed the large chef's knife from the block of wood within his grasp, the blade gleamed invitingly.

He heard his mother scream as he lunged at Krone, his eyes raving with indiscretion.

With the opposite hand, Derrick grabbed ahold of his suit and shoved him back, against the counter, shoving the blade of the knife against his father's throat.

"Let's see how well you fare when I'm not chained up like a fucking animal!" Derrick screamed, pushing the blade deeper into his throat, forcing the old man to back up.

However, instead of seeing the fear that Derrick hoped to evoke, the same fear that was present in Lily's eyes as she died, Krone's eyes gleamed. His smug expression intensified as though he was taking great pleasure in dragging his son to such a desperate low.

"You know as well as I do that you are no more than a single body away from being booked for murder..." His lips tugged upwards, revealing his perfectly white, yet strangely sharp teeth.

Derrick's rage instantly intensified. He gripped harder on the handle of the knife with every intention of slicing the blade clean against Krone's carotid artery and watching the bastard bleed out, right there on the kitchen floor.

Yet, before he could execute the slice, Derrick felt his mother grab his shoulder and thrust him back.

"Derrick, no!" She wailed as she yanked at him.

Karen wasn't strong enough to do all that much damage, but she was able to distract him for a moment, which was plenty of time for Krone to retaliate.

Almost at the same time as Derrick felt the diversion snap his attention away from his goal, he felt the hand with the knife be pushed back. Before he could react, Krone had slipped out of his grasp and he was shoved against the counter, with his arm wrenching painfully up his back.

Derrick attempted to fight back, but as he picked his head up, he felt a needle jam into his neck. Liquid flowed freely and rapidly into his vein, instantly causing him to feel out of touch with reality.

His eyes became unfocused and his limbs once again felt heavy.

Once again, he heard his mother yell out with fear and confusion as he fought to keep his eyes opened.

However, before he could assemble enough strength to fight back, the world, as fuzzy and distorted as it had become, went completely black.

Derrick didn't even feel himself hit the ground.

Chapter 17

Upon waking up, Derrick realized that he was still in the same place he was rendered unconscious.

He was aware of that fact even before he opened his eyes. He felt the tile against his cheek and the grout gliding across his fingertips. His back ached from lying on something hard and his body was contorted in a strange position.

Krone had literally dropped him there.

However, when he opened his eyes, he realized that both his mother and Krone had left in a hurry.

The house felt almost as eerie as his own. He knew, instinctively, that no one else was there. Every presence, save for his own had vacated the house before he had even started to come around.

In his transition out of unconsciousness, he hadn't heard so much as a hurried footstep, or a slamming door, signaling he was alone for a while. He had a knack for remembering such details and as far as he could tell, none of them were present.

After taking stock of his injuries and figuring it didn't much matter at this point anyway, he hurriedly pushed himself up, off the floor. When he did, he felt something small drop off of his person and tap rapidly against the floor before growing silent.

At first, Derrick thought his phone had fallen out of his pocket, even though the sound didn't quite match up. Yet, when he looked around, he saw a flash drive sitting on the floor between his feet.

Oh God...Not again... He thought, instantly feeling sick as he reached down to pick up the USB.

When he reached back up, his eyes searched over the familiar house for any sign of a computer; preferably one that he didn't mind breaking.

If this message came with the same encryption as the other two, any technology used to view the files that the drive contained would be destroyed.

Derrick settled on the television that his mother would routinely watch soap operas on, instead of focusing on her family and the drama that ensued all around her.

He wished he could gain some kind of satisfaction from that, but he was far too concerned with what terrible message his father had waiting for him to worry about spiting his mother.

Trying not to overthink what he was in store for, he connected the hard drive and turned on the television.

Immediately, Krone's face filled his view.

His expression was disgustingly simple, as though he had waited for this moment for a lifetime.

Derrick tried to look in the background, to figure out any clues as to where Krone was since it was obvious he wasn't in either his or his mother's house.

However, he was sure that he had never been there before.

The lighting was dim and the walls were cemented. The floor was dirt. Wooden beams made up the rafters and the filth that accompanied the dirt floor was overly apparent.

It appeared to be some kind of old, likely abandoned cellar.

The surroundings were innately disturbing, but even for effect, this didn't seem like a place Krone would even be caught dead.

"I apologize for this not being in person, but time constraints prevent it. I am a busy man, as you know. However, your attempt on my life has left me with little recourse."

Derrick narrowed his eyes, feeling his body start to shake, even before he was sure of what was going on. His stomach churned nervously.

"I have had ample time to conduct my experiments and I believe that the following demonstration will illustrate my findings quite succinctly." He stopped to sneer into the camera, his eyes glistened with a morbid sense of egregious satisfaction. "While you were sleeping off the effects of my mere self-defense, a cowardly attempt on your part, I decided to show you exactly what it means to cross me."

With that, the camera zoomed out and Eva came into focus, being led down the stairs by another one of Krone's henchmen.

What have I done? He thought, feeling like he was going to throw up.

Seeing her, his knees felt weak. The knowledge that no matter what happened, he would be forced to watch, with absolutely no chance of being able to stop it.

The knowledge that whatever this video contained already took place tore him up.

Eva took stock of her surroundings. She looked confused and dazed. Her movements were sluggish and Derrick wondered if she was drugged.

"What's going on?" Eva demanded. "Where are we?"

"I have not been completely honest with you, Eva."

"I know." She spat, eyeing the camera as though she had a good idea what it was being used for.

"I didn't want to hurt you further." He exclaimed. "I tried to tell you that your mother and father abandoned you, but that's not entirely true."

"I know." She insisted. "Just let me go home." As she said that, she bit her bottom lip, trying hard to contain her emotion. "Please?"

"I'm sorry...I can't do that." Krone told her and as he turned towards her the dim lighting illuminated a revolver in his hand. "In truth, your father hired me to do a job."

She shook her head and started to back up.

"No..." She insisted as her fear got the best of her. "You're lying. My Mom and Dad love me. You're evil." She insisted with narrowed eyes. "What's the camera for?"

"I know it's difficult for you to understand, but your father...he wants proof. Unfortunately, he wouldn't take my word for it, or this wouldn't be necessary."

"No..." Derrick hissed, his eyes growing wide. His fists clenched and his jaw tightened.

"You're lying!" She screamed as tears started to stream down her face.

She turned to run but the man who had led her down the stairs stepped in her path. He grabbed her and turned her around to face Krone.

She tried to back up, but the man kept her still. She struggled for a moment, but eventually stopped, breathing heavily as though exhausted.

Derrick wanted to look away. He wanted to turn it off, but he couldn't. He needed to know what happened to his daughter.

"Eva..." He breathed, drawing closer to the television, loathing himself for not being there to save her, to comfort her and to assure her that all he ever did was try to protect her.

When Krone produced the gun, Eva screamed and cowered away from him as much as her captor would allow.

"Please..." She begged. "Don't..."

However, when her pleas fell on deaf ears, she looked directly at the camera.

Derrick's jaw hinged and his body shook. He felt himself be overcome by emotions as the conclusion to his worst nightmare played out before his eyes.

Once again, he was completely powerless to stop it.

"Daddy! I know you love me..." Her voice was hurried and her eyes darted back and forth between the camera and the gun. "He's a bad man." She insisted as fear overwhelmed her. "I'm sorry. I love you too..."

With that, the gun went off and after a quick shriek of terror, Eva's voice ceased completely.

"No!" Derrick cried as he watched her fall to the ground, completely motionless. Immediately, all of his remaining strength was zapped. He sank to his knees as he screamed in agony.

Derrick felt completely numb and engorged by rage and pain all at the same time.

Everything and nothing culminated together to create a cataclysmic explosion of vexation.

He couldn't think. Didn't want to think.

He wanted to escape reality entirely, without ever looking back. He hated this world, himself and everything that was forced upon him.

This is all my fault... He told himself, breathing heavy, panting breaths, the execution of which did nothing to oxygenate his distraught mind.

Once again, he felt as though he couldn't breathe. It felt as though a noose was tightening around his throat, closing off his airway and causing his mind to shut down.

He could hear the hastened beating of his heart and he could feel the pumping of his boiling blood as it coursed rapidly through his body, trying to flush out the perceived threat.

However, the noose was threaded with nothing more than his own failure. Having struck again, now to take everything he loved away from him, it constricted him, shredding him apart from the inside out.

Yet, the cruelest part about the torment wrought from his own mind was that regardless of how much pain and suffering he endured, no matter what he did from this point forward, nothing could bring them back.

His family was now lost to him forever.

Shattered, he threw his body down on the floor and pounded his fist against the carpet.

Part of him wanted to destroy everything he could get his hands on and burn the house down with him inside, while part of him simply begged the pain and suffering that consumed him to kill him now.

Either way, as he looked up again to the sight of Eva lying face down in a dark, growing puddle of blood, he knew that one way or another, he too was going to die.

Chapter 18

Eric didn't like the idea of leaving. In fact, he hated it.

Therefore, he had decided that he simply wasn't going to go. He'd be damned if he left his brother now when he needed him the most.

When his mother had called to tell him to get right home, that their plane was leaving in a few hours, he had told her he wasn't going. He had explained that he thought leaving Derrick was a mistake and she had the audacity to try to tell him she was trying to protect him.

He had no words after that. So, he simply hung up and texted one of his friends to come and get him; that he needed a ride to his brother's house.

While he waited on the corner, he paced back and forth, stewing about everything that had gone on over the course of the last week.

Every waking moment he thought about how terrible he felt for Derrick and his family.

Yet, despite being visited by the police and being part of a search party to Lily and Eva, which obviously came up empty, it still didn't feel real.

Perhaps it was simply that he was in denial, or maybe it was the sheer volume of atrocities that took place in such a short period of time. Whatever it was, though, Eric had a hard time coming to grips with it.

However, the more he analyzed how he felt, the harder it was to imagine what Derrick was going through. After all, he had seen it all. It was his fiancée and daughter.

Still, he managed to keep it together, both with his lie and personally, behind closed doors.

He knew that Derrick was hanging on a meager strand of hope, but even the fact that he had managed to hold onto anything was a miracle.

Now this... Eric thought, shaking his head and wishing that Krone had actually put him in danger, instead of simply using him as a decoy to attack Lily and Eva. *At least I can take care of myself.* He thought bitterly.

He didn't look up at first when he heard a car roll up to the curb and stop.

It was too quick for his friend to have arrived and so he thought that it was merely a coincidence that the car stopped here.

However, when he turned and his eye caught a flash of pristine black, stretch limousine, Eric looked up and focused hard on the car. The tinted windows glared back at him, shielding the identity of the person inside completely.

This can't be... He thought. *They're long gone by now.*

His thought was to run, knowing that no good could come of this interaction, but before he could turn around, he felt the barrel of a gun jab him in the back.

Eric sighed and rolled his eyes.

"Get in the car." A man's voice commanded.

"Go ahead. Shoot me." Eric taunted, but instead, the door to the back of the limo opened and he was roughly shoved inside.

When he tried to fight, he was reprimanded with the butt of the gun, smacking him in the back of the head.

In the daze that caught him off-guard, he fell forward and was wrestled into submission by the man with the gun and an accomplice who was still in the car.

One man held him face down while the other jabbed a knee in his back and bound his hands behind him with rope.

Eventually, Eric stopped struggling and focused on making it easier on himself to get free once he had the opportunity.

"You know, all of this wouldn't be necessary if you were more cooperative." A voice from his past, that he had only heard recently one other time sneered as Eric was yanked into a sitting position.

The moment Eric's gaze fell on his father, sitting on the row of crimson, leather seats across from him, rage exploded inside of him.

"You fucking psychopath!" Eric screamed, throwing all of his weight behind trying to leap at Krone.

Immediately, the two men who had captured him before grabbed ahold of his shoulders and slammed him back against the seat.

However, Eric kept fighting.

"The second I get the chance; I am going to murder you."

"Your brother tried that already today. It didn't end too well for him." Krone answered in a bored tone.

"What did you do to him?" Eric demanded, snarling with bared teeth, still struggling to get to him.

"I convinced him that his daughter was dead...With the help of movie magic, coupled with his fragile emotional state, I'm confident that I was able to convince him that I killed her."

Eric felt as though all of the air was forced from his lungs as his stomach plummeted.

"You bastard! Why can't you just leave him alone?" He growled, trying to hide the emotion that was welling up inside of him. The anger and resentment made him crazy while the empathy he had for his brother made him irrational.

"A word of advice for when you try to kill me, as I have no doubt that you will, finish the job, or you will not like my retaliation."

At this, Eric stopped struggling. He peered at Krone in an attempt to decipher what it was he was truly telling him.

"But, she's not dead? You lied to him." He decided.

"Well, of course, I lied to him."

"Then, where is she?"

"Not dead." His snicker was morbid and daunting. "At least, not yet."

As they spoke, Eric focused on discretely working with the ropes to free his hands.

"What do you want with Eva? Was this all simply to hurt Derrick?"

"When have I ever been so one-dimensional?" He retorted. "Certainly, watching Derrick squirm helplessly as I slaughtered the woman he loved like a swine before the Christmas feast was amusing, but that wasn't my only motivation."

Eric bared his teeth and glowered at his father, but refrained from leaping at him again, for fear of being unable to gain more information.

"I believe that your mother has informed you that we will be moving to California. I am here to ensure you make it on your flight."

"Where is Eva?" Eric snarled.

"Oh, she's already there. I've arranged for some...associates to take care of her while I am dealing with you."

With a flick of the wrist, Eric finally was able to slide a loop of the rope off of his wrist. As long as he wasn't caught, he would be able to free himself fully at any moment.

"If you hurt her..."

"Oh, I wouldn't worry about her getting hurt." He narrowed his eyes at him. "You see; I have a plan for her. For now, she believes her parents abandoned her, but eventually, I will tell her that her mother is, in fact, dead and that her Daddy killed her.   Which...isn't   completely inaccurate..."

"You're the only one who's responsible for Lily's death," Eric growled, realizing that the more Krone spoke, the harder it was to control himself.

"Though the embellishment of him enlisting your help would be solely a manner of fanning that vengeful fire, you know..." Before giving Eric even a moment to respond, he chuckled and leaned in, closer to him, with provocation heavily dictating his movements. "Speaking of your dear brother, how is he going to take your disappearance? That has got to hurt. After everything he's done to protect you, only so that you can be forced right back into the clutches of the man who has already taken so much from him." He sighed as his eyebrows raised.

Eric swallowed hard, his eyes piercing deeply into his father's, wishing that he could get free long enough to hurt him like he had hurt his sons.

"It's dangerous, bringing me with you. You can't kill me, so I'll just be a liability. I will never stop searching for Eva." He promised him.

"Perhaps you will be your niece's first kill." He mused with scornful intent, almost as though he hadn't heard a word Eric had said.

At this, Eric let out a bellowing, humorless laugh.

"You and I both know that if you could kill me, you would've done it a long time ago."

"Fair enough." Krone insisted with a nod. "However, when I have unrestrained access to you, without any hope of interference it will be a great asset to me." His eyes gleamed with the presentation of a challenge. "There is a way to kill you. I am sure of it. However, until I figure it out, I am going to put you through hell."

Eric narrowed his eyes defiantly.

"While I might not know how to kill you, I am sure that you feel pain." Within the pointed pause, the man with the gun smashed the butt of the gun across Eric's face, causing him to inadvertently yell out.

"Hence, my methods will leave you wishing you could die on a daily basis; all for the sake of my research." Krone continued as though nothing had happened. "It might not take long before you actually start helping me decipher the meaning to your end, simply so that the pain I am inflicting upon you will finally stop." After letting his words sink in, Krone leaned in closer to Eric, narrowing his eyes and lowering his tone to a sadistic hiss. "And once again, there won't be a thing your brother will be able to do to stop me. Seems to have become his mantra, no?"

Eric drew in a deep, calming breath, trying not to show any weakness.

"Though, I will find a way to keep your brother apprised of our progress." He chuckled. "Once I have decoded your cipher, though, I will allow his daughter to take out her disdain on her uncle." He pressed. "After grooming Eva against you, embedding the same hatred for your brother and for you that I would imagine you have for me, I doubt it will be all that difficult. Therefore, when she kills you, her intentions will manifest from a place far deeper than what is evoked throughout a simple assignment. This will be personal. She will be killing her uncle, the only person on the planet that believes Derrick innocent, more to hurt her father than to hurt you and when she does, Derrick will be the first to know."

His shoulders rose and lowered with egregious mockery. "Who knows...He might even get to share in your final moments...If he even makes it that long without throwing himself off a building or something." He chuckled knowingly.

"Fuck you!" Eric hissed, propelling himself forward.

This time, as he was being shoved back, he felt the limousine coming to a stop.

Not sure where they were going, Eric wasn't sure how many more opportunities he would have to escape.

As much as he wanted to make Krone suffer, he needed to tell Derrick that Eva was alive before it was too late.

So, taking advantage of the men trying to subdue him, Eric slipped the rest of the way out of the ropes and immediately grabbed for the gun.

Catching the man off guard, he grabbed it and swung back, hitting the man behind him in the bridge of the nose.

While Krone and the other man reached for a weapon, Eric went for the door. Finding it was locked, he shot it, which caused the driver to slam on the breaks, jostling everyone in the car.

Eric was thrown backward and grabbed from behind by the man who had originally persuaded him to get in the car.

Kicking his feet out, Eric was able to throw opened the damaged car door. Once he saw that he had a chance of getting free, he wrestled out of the man's grasp and leaped at the door.

He felt Krone grab his arm and try to inject him with something, but he quickly tore his arm away, breaking the needle.

Eric felt the snap reverberate through his arm, but his adrenaline was coursing too rapidly to let anything stop him.

Knowing that he only had a moment, Eric dove forward, hoping that he would make it out of the car.

To his ultimate surprise, he felt the sting of asphalt singe his entire body as he rolled and skid against it.

However, Eric knew that he didn't have time for pain. All he needed to do right now was get away from that limousine.

So, as soon as he was able, he stopped himself from moving and got to his feet. The moment he was standing straight up, he took off towards a patch of woods that he saw.

Behind him, he could hear the limo turning around. The tires screeched and the engine roared as it raced back towards him.

With a stroke of luck, Eric was able to duck into the trees before the vehicle made it back to him.

Chancing a look behind him, he saw the car pull over to the side of the road and the two thugs jump out of the back.

Now, they were both garnishing weapons, but as secluded as they seemed to be, it would still be stupid for them to fire off a shot. Unless it was perfect, he was fairly certain the guns would be useless to them now.

Realizing this, Eric crouched low and moved quickly, trying to throw them off of his path. He figured they would be able to track him, but he hoped to find a ride before he needed to slow down enough to be in danger of them finding him.

After all, Derrick had taught him well. He felt prepared, as strange as that sounded and thus, the only true fear on his mind was the hope that he wasn't too late.

Chapter 19

Derrick watched as the last of the ice cube melted into his dark amber drink. Three-quarters of the way through a handle of Jack Daniels, his hazy eyes moved past the tumbler and settled on the .357 revolver sitting amongst the remanence of his liquid grief.

He thought about picking it up. He wondered how long it would take him to do the deed, once he finally held it in his grasp. He had no doubt that he would be able to accomplish his goal.

At this point, it was only a matter of when.

Had he not experienced a brief intermission of happiness, which led him to the worst, most destructive heartbreak, beyond anything he could have ever fathomed, he probably would have done this a long time ago, but for far less of a reason.

He knew the gun was loaded and in his drunken stupor, he welcomed the weight of it, resting in his palm as he imagined pressing the barrel against his temple and pulling the trigger. Cool metal heating up with a final thought before the darkness consumed him.

His only remaining hope for salvation.

Probably won't even fucking feel it. He thought, overwhelmed with an even greater sense of defeat.

Still, Derrick wanted to forget.

He was only plagued by the memories of his failure for a few days and already it was driving him completely insane.

Of course, the alcohol didn't help.

Concluding he was still sober enough to realize that, he ditched the tumbler and grasped a firm grip on the handle itself. Warm, burning singed his throat as he thrust the handle up over his head and chugged the remainder of the bottle in only a few slugs.

When he had bled the bottle dry, he glowered at the glass as though it had betrayed him and tossed it aside.

Somewhere on the other side of the room, he heard the glass break and a burning, hateful ire consumed him.

Jealousy at the destruction of the bottle before he took his own life, rocketed through him.

With a wistful expression, his eyes wavered towards his daughter's room.

Through his intoxication, the memory of the terrible events that took place only a week before were the only clear thoughts he had. It was almost as though his own mind was turning against him, taunting him.

He was so drunk, his present gaze caused everything in its path to swish and swirl as though he was in some kind of sadistic funhouse. Yet, the memories of how he lost his family; they remained crystal clear.

No matter how much he consumed, the memories never dulled and that only made him angrier, crazier and more horrified.

Each time his mind forced him to relive it, he knew that he was lifetimes away from his own sanity.

Realizing this and knowing he was ready, Derrick reached forward and grabbed hold of the gun. The weight of it was nothing, compared to the weight of the secret that he held and the guilt of having his family's blood on his hands.

In a way, holding the firearm in his hand was disappointing. He had thought, in his drunken stupor, the implication of the gun, once he brought it close to him, would mean something more.

Then again, to him, his life no longer meant anything, so why should the method he used to dispose of it hold any overarching significance?

He drew in a deep breath; confident it would be one of his last. As he did so, he pulled the revolver up to his head and pressed the barrel against his temple.

The pressure of the weapon also fell short. He thought it would hurt more. He was under the assumption that, before he pulled the trigger, he would recognize the weight of what he was about to do.

Yet, that sense of self-worth, as trivial as it was to anyone but him never came.

Somewhere within his preparations, Derrick thought he heard the sound of a door. Although, he was far too gone to care.

If someone was coming to try to kill him, they would certainly be too late. He was beyond giving anyone else the satisfaction of taking his life.

The determination of when he would take his last breath was quite literally the only thing he had left.

He'd be damned if he allowed anyone to take it from him.

Thus, he pressed the barrel deeper into his temple and closed his eyes for a moment to ward off the wave of overwhelming dizziness and intoxication that plagued him.

When he opened his eyes again, however, he found that Eric had materialized in front of him.

He stood before him, looking slightly confused, but he wasn't panicking or doing anything at all to stop him. This led Derrick to wonder if Eric was actually there, or if this was simply another trick that his mind had concocted to hurt him deeper.

Although, his disappointed expression led Derrick to momentarily second-guess what he was doing.

Whether he was actually there or not, he couldn't bring himself to force his brother to watch him die, like he had been forced to watch Lily die.

Regardless of what he felt about himself and how desperately he wanted to end his life, he wouldn't want to wish his torment on anyone; least of all his brother.

Derrick felt the gun drop, away from his head and come to rest on his knee. He kept his finger securely on the trigger but had no intention of using the weapon until he was alone.

That is, not unless he had to.

"What the hell are you doing here?" He slurred, narrowing his eyes at Eric, still expecting him to try to foil his plan.

"I came to check on you. You weren't answering your phone." Eric replied, still refraining from coming any closer or making any sudden movements.

"Well, now that you know what I'm up to, leave me alone...Unless you've come here to stop me." His voice sounded threatening, but in reality, he was desperate. He knew that if he wanted to, Eric could easily overpower him, ruining his escape.

Already, he was feeling the culmination of the alcohol truly taking ahold of him. If he waited too much longer, the poison he used to facilitate his suicide would be his undoing.

Therefore, he had to convince Eric to leave quickly, while he was still basically remained in control of his body.

"No." Eric shook his head and drew in a troubled breath. Still, his voice remained articulate and understanding. "You've been through a lot...I can't even begin to imagine how you're feeling. If I were you, I might not have even made it this far."

"Good. I'm glad you understand. Now get out."

Eric raised his hands, as though in surrender and started to back up.

"Alright. I will, but first, can I ask you a question?" He didn't wait for an answer. "If you die, who's going to raise Eva?"

"Eva's dead." Derrick blurted, now too drunk out of his mind to care about his own feelings. It isn't like he could hurt anymore.

He knew she was dead. Whether he said it aloud or not didn't change that.

"No, Derrick...She isn't."

Derrick narrowed his eyes in confusion but wanted to believe. He knew that Eric wouldn't lie to him.

However, he was completely under the impression that his brother was misinformed.

"I know what Krone did. He faked her death." Eric insisted, as though his face explained everything he was thinking. "He lied to you. He told me when he thought that I was going with him." This time, he took a step towards Derrick with insistence. "I swear to God, she's alive. Put down the gun and we'll find her together."

Derrick knew, even though the haze of his intoxication, that he had a choice. Feeling the effects of the alcohol starting to consume him, he realized that unconsciousness was only mere moments away.

If he was going to follow through with his intentions, he was going to have to do it now, whether Eric was there or not.

His unfocused eyes did their best to peer deeply into Eric's gaze, trying to decide what his next and possibly final move should be.

Derrick drew in a deep breath, allowed it to clear his otherwise sloshing thoughts and with the exhale, he dropped the gun, subsequently passing out.

The next morning, Derrick awoke to the smell of coffee.

Immediately, his head hurt and his insides felt jittery. His stomach churned uncomfortably and his eyes felt heavy.

"Get up! You've got a long drive." Eric's voice barely penetrated through the wall of disorientation that his hangover had wrought, but when it did, the sound was nearly unbearable.

"God, Eric...Not so damn loud..." He hissed, grasping his head in his hand. After he had a moment to collect himself, he opened one eye to find that he was still in the recliner he had passed out in, with the gun still lying next to him.

In front of him, Eric had set up a large cup of coffee, some Gatorade and a few tablets of Aspirin.

"Come on! We'll get breakfast on the way. Something greasy...That'll coat your stomach...Make you feel better."

The thought of food in general, much less anything greasy made Derrick's stomach churn.

"I'd much rather have the hair of the dog..."

"Well, you can't, because you have to drive and that's the last thing we need..."

"Drive where?" He grumbled.

"California. I figured out where Krone lives and I figured we can start there. Although, I don't think Eva is with him, specifically. I think she's with caretakers of his property that live close to his house."

Derrick glared at Eric with confusion as his stomach threatened to betray him.

"And...you know where this house is?"

"I have a pretty good idea." He answered with confidence that automatically morphed into annoyance when Derrick looked as though he might demand more information from him. "Come on! The sooner we get on the road, the sooner we can get to Eva."

Chapter 20

The truck sped west on Interstate 70 with unwavering intent as Derrick listened to his brother recount exactly what had happened the day before.

The wrappers from the cheesesteaks and fries whipped around the back as the interstate air blew through the truck through the opened windows. Attached to the dashboard, his phone's GPS plotted a course for a nearly 44-hour trip to a cove on the secluded outskirts of Monterey Bay, California.

The night before, Eric was able to dig up some purchasing records for a mansion that was sold about ten years ago to a wealthy psychologist, named Dr. Alexander Krone.

Old photos of the property showed that there was also a house in the back that was meant to be living quarters for the hired help.

For whatever reason, Eric thought that Eva was being held there. His explanation was that while it might raise a few eyebrows if a child suddenly appeared in the main house, he could literally hide her away in this house, since it was secluded and inaccessible from the road, without going through the property.

Since it was the best lead they had, Derrick went along with it, hoping that by some miracle, Eric was right.

"So, let me get this straight..." Derrick demanded, his expression doubtful. "He just told you all of this?"

"Yeah!" Eric chuckled. "Dumbass. I guess he thought I wouldn't be able to get the information back to you."

"Or he knew you would..." Derrick sounded doubtful as he chanced a glance across the truck, towards his little brother.

"What?" He demanded, narrowing his eyes. It was obvious from the tone of his voice that he hadn't thought about the possibility and that frightened him. "Why would he want to do that?"

"Perhaps he hasn't quite gotten his fill of making my life a living hell," Derrick responded with a nonchalant rise and fall of his shoulders, while his eyes focused on the road. His jaw tightened, but otherwise, he felt nothing more than a slow simmer of rage.

Inside, Derrick felt brutally gutted and left to die. Unfortunately for him, death never came.

He tried to be positive and hold out hope that Eric's information was correct; that Eva was still alive, but aside from delaying his suicide until he was sure, he found it difficult to feel anything more. If he were to see her, things would be different and even with his uncertainty, he wasn't going to stop. If this was a trap, there wasn't much more Krone could do to him.

After all, dead is dead and while it would obliterate what was left of him to see Eva or Lily's body, it wouldn't change anything. The knowledge that they were dead had already done its damage.

Now, anything that Krone could do would only add more justification this his decision.

Eric was quiet for a long, strained moment.

"No." He finally argued. "Krone told me all of that stuff, thinking that for whatever reason, it would be too late. He was almost convinced that you had already killed yourself. He made it sound like he was banking on it, driving you to do it. He thought he had me and Eva all to himself."

"I don't know. Krone isn't the type to leave something like that for fate to decide. If he wanted me dead, why didn't he kill me himself?"

"Because he knew that he was right." Eric retorted, sounding slightly angry at the insinuation that he was leading Derrick into even more torment. "Might I remind you that I walked in on you with a gun to your head? I mean, if I had gotten to your house five minutes later, it would've been too late."

"Yeah. You're right." He admitted, unable to look at him. He wasn't ashamed of what he had tried to do. If the information he was given proved to be false, he wouldn't hesitate to do it again, but the sound of Eric's voice told him that he should care far more than he did.

"So, then what makes you think that he's lying? If he thought you were dead, what would the point of taunting me about it be if I was going to find out the truth anyway?"

"Leverage? Screw with your head? Who the hell knows..." He grumbled, not particularly fond of continuing this conversation any longer.

"I don't think that's it...At least, not entirely." Eric insisted. "Of course, you know, threatening to have my niece eventually kill me was probably to mess with my head, but that would be an idol threat if Eva's dead...and that sounds more unrealistic. He has built an underworld empire on making good on his threats."

Derrick considered this but decided against commenting.

"If you don't believe me, why are we still going?" Eric finally demanded, after the silence finally agitated him enough.

"Because not knowing is far worse than being sure." He responded, almost immediately. "I'd do anything in the world to find her. If there's even a chance that she might still be alive, I'd follow the trail anywhere."

"Well, for what it's worth, I wouldn't have put you through all of this if I didn't genuinely believe that there was still a hope of finding her..."

"I know." He assured. "But I guarantee that Krone would."

"You're right. He would and if that's the case..."

"Forget it." He interrupted him, shooting Eric a look of warning, silently forbidding him to continue.

Heeding the warning, his brother hastily changed the subject.

"So, when you get Eva back, what are you going to do?"

"I'm sure as hell not going to go back to the house. I can't." His shoulders rose and fell with a certain degree of uncertainty. "I guess we'll have to hide.

Now that I know Krone does actually want her for her abilities, I need to stay one step ahead of him. Hopefully, though, we can disappear into some city and I can give Eva something of a normal life."

"Has she ever shown any signs of having abilities?" Eric's voice was somewhat apologetic, though Derrick wasn't sure why.

They might not have spoken much about the abilities that have both fueled and maintained the life they have had to live, but they never denied their existence. They were both aware that their children could possess the abilities as well and if Krone's hypothesis was correct, those abilities would be far more advanced than theirs.

"She's smart...resourceful." He answered.

"But to the best of my knowledge, she's never moved anything across the room with her mind or levitated. Nothing out of the ordinary."

"I wasn't anything special either, though." Eric reminded him.

This comment annoyed Derrick.

"Yeah, well, if she has your ability or anything like it, maybe Krone was telling us both the truth after all."

Chapter 21

Fifty-three hours after leaving the house, stopping only for gas, food and a few hours of sleep, the truck drove down the road that was supposed to lead them to the mansion bought by Dr. Alexander Krone.

The shells cracked underneath the tires as they pulled up the long, winding driveway.

"Dude, what are you doing?" Eric asked, peering out the windshield as they wound through the trees lining either side of their narrow path.

"I'm driving?" Derrick hissed. "What the hell does it look like I'm doing?"

It seemed that the closer they got to their destination, the angrier Derrick became.

Eric had observed this change a few hundred miles back but didn't comment on it. Instead, he simply tried to dodge as many of the inevitable sinkholes in their conversations as possible; attempting to limit his brother's frustrations.

After all, he was the one driving and in his fragile state, Eric recognized how detrimental of a decision that could be for both of them. So, he did his best to keep Derrick's temper from flaring.

Now that they were approaching the mansion which hopefully held his daughter, hopefully, alive and well, anything Eric said seemed to trigger a viscerally explosive reaction.

"Right." Eric hissed, trying his best not to roll his eyes. "I'm only saying that maybe you should...you know, not drive right up to the front gate."

"I'm not!" He insisted as he cut the wheel sharply, turning off the shell-streamed path and rattling through a patch of trees.

Wondering seriously if Derrick had decided once again that the endeavor was useless, Eric braced himself.

"What the hell!" He screamed, grabbing onto the armrest and the dashboard as the truck bounced up and down on the uneven ground, barely squeezing between the trees that lined its path.

Sure that they were going to hit something at any moment, Eric shut his eyes, not wanting to see whatever it was that was guaranteed to seal his fate.

Even though ultimately, the crash wouldn't kill him, that didn't mean that it wouldn't hurt like hell.

Yet, before that fatal blow ever came, the truck came screeching to a halt with such an abrupt force, it knocked Eric forward.

"Seriously?" He demanded, glaring at Derrick when the truck finally stopped quivering from such an abrupt stop.

"Let's go," Derrick replied, his face grim and emotionless.

"Wait a minute!" Eric exclaimed as Derrick threw opened his truck door and jumped down. "What was that?"

"That was me ensuring that I could make a getaway out of a hiding spot," Derrick answered as he pulled the front seat forward and dug out the revolver he had planned to shoot himself with the night before. Sticking it in his sweatshirt pocket, he looked up at Eric as if to demand the entirety of his questions.

"We cannot leave this way." Eric insisted, peering through the thick over-brush of trees and weeds that flourished in the pristine California weather.

"Trust me. We'll be fine. I noticed on the map there was a path and when I saw it, I was fairly certain that we could get the truck through it."

"Fairly certain?" Eric hissed.

Derrick's shoulders rose up and fell with a confrontational edge.

"You're fairly certain Krone didn't actually kill my daughter in front of me, the least you can do is humor my ability to know how to get her the hell out of here if indeed we do find her."

Eric wasn't exactly sure how to take that, but as Derrick slid another handgun across the seat towards him and slammed the door, he figured that the conversation was over.

Grabbing the gun and slamming the door himself, he hurried to catch up to Derrick, not wanting to lose him in the dense thicket of unusual wildlife that surrounded the mansion.

Following close behind his brother, Eric couldn't help but fear that he had made a mistake, bringing Derrick out here.

Obviously, he still didn't fully believe that Eva was alive. Plus, even if she was still alive, if Krone had any time at all to prepare for their arrival, they could be walking right into a trap.

He was terrified of what they would find when they snuck their way onto the grounds. However, his concern had little to do with his own wellbeing and far more to do with Derrick's.

After everything that had happened, he couldn't bear to think about his brother getting hurt again.

Yet, playing every scenario through his head, from being doomed from the start to having a fair chance, he couldn't think of a realistic, ideal situation.

They didn't have a plan and the only goal they had even remotely constructed was to save Eva; if that was still even a possibility.

Not to mention, if it wasn't, Derrick might never forgive Eric for dragging him all the way out here for yet another devastating blow. He couldn't blame him, though. Eric knew that if he was wrong, he would have a hard time forgiving himself.

He wanted to talk to Derrick about this and he had tried to multiple times during the trip, but he hadn't wanted to hear it. He was all in, no matter what and if for some reason Eva had died, Derrick had convinced himself he had no further reason to live.

While Eric couldn't blame him, he also wished there was something he could do to change his mind. He would've done anything to save his life, but he was steadfast in the belief that without Lily or Eva, his life didn't matter.

Eric knew that Derrick blamed himself for what happened, but from the outside looking in, he knew that there was no way he could've known Krone's intentions.

When Derrick found Lily, Eric was happy that his older brother was doing something for himself.

The news that they were expecting had only solidified what Eric had already thought. He was finally living his own life. It was great. They were both naive in thinking that they had the luxury of building a normal life, but even after everything that had happened, Eric still couldn't say that his brother did the wrong thing.

He loved his family and wanted the best for them. He deserved to have that happiness in his life, even as short-lived as it might have been.

Unfortunately, Eric couldn't think of a way to convince him of that. However, the more the two of them walked, the more Eric became convinced that Derrick wasn't thinking clearly.

He didn't blame him. In fact, he was surprised that he was thinking as clearly as he was, but eventually, it became clear that he had to do something, or neither one of them stood a chance.

"Hey, Der...Derrick, can I talk to you about something?" Eric called, reaching out to stop his brother.

Derrick spun around, almost as though he was ready for a fight. However, noticing it was Eric, the fire in his eyes burned to a cinder.

"What?" He demanded.

"Do you have a plan? I mean, I'm all for going in there all Terminator style, but this isn't a suicide mission. It's a rescue."

"We hope." He spat bitterly, but Eric could see that his concern had provoked a more rational way of thinking. Even though he was positive Derrick wouldn't admit it, he watched his eyes trace the ground as he worked out a plan in his head.

Eric remained quiet, hoping he was thinking about a plan and not a way to ditch him because he was afraid he was trying to chicken out on him.

"There was a diner down the road a ways, right?" Derrick asked.

"Yeah?"

"I know. I saw it on the way in…. We can get there and back quicker through the woods."

"Why? Does the thought of a rescue mission make you crave pie or something?"

"No." He snapped. "Shut up!"

With that, Derrick fell back into thought before finally staring back at Eric and revealing his thoughts.

"You're right. We need a better plan. We'll break in and take a look around. The gate is right up there. Once we've decided what we're dealing with, we'll walk to the diner and make a plan. Then, we'll come back."

"So, a recon mission?" Eric asked in a far more thankful tone than he intended.

Derrick stared at him for a moment before shaking his head.

"No more talking, unless you have something important to say."

With that, he took off towards the gate.

"Well, screw you too." Eric hissed, glaring at his brother's back before following in his shadow.

By the time they reached the fence, darkness was descending upon the mansion, which made their father's fortress even creepier. Yet, the cover was convenient.

Scaling the fence, despite its harrowing, wrought iron presence, came easily to both of them. Once they were on the right side of it, under the cloak of darkness, they made a dash for the guest house that sat behind the main building.

The lights shining in the windows not only illuminated their path but also helped them to determine that it was likely someone was present inside the house.

When they reached the building, they crept close to it, careful not to be noticed and decided to chance a look into a nearby window.

Derrick stood up, bracing himself against the wall and turned his head so that he could see what was going on inside.

Eric watched as he peered cautiously, before leaning in closer.

"Oh my God..." He hissed in a tone that was too low for Eric to decipher.

A leap of fear caused his heart to thump wildly in his chest.

"What's the matter?" Eric demanded.

"She's here." He responded. "Eva's alive!" He exclaimed. "I have to get her!"

As he lurched forward, Eric sprang into action.

Hastily, he caught Derrick and pushed him back into the shadow of the building.

"What are you doing?" Eric demanded. "Remember the plan? We're going to go to the diner, map out a strategy and..."

"To hell with strategy. She's right there!" He insisted, his eyes narrowing with disbelief as he tried to muscle himself away from Eric.

"Derrick, think about this!" He insisted, trying to appeal to the part of him that was not bound by all of the terrible emotions Eric was sure his brother was experiencing. "If you go in there now, with no plan, you'll die...or worse, Eva might really get killed."

"Yeah, well unless you can guarantee she won't get hurt with your plan, then I don't want her to be in there with those fuckers for another second." He snarled, his eyes practically glowing red with ire.

"I know!" Eric insisted. "Neither do I...and I can't guarantee anything but the fact that going in there right now is a stupid idea."

"There's caretakers in there. A man and a woman. I don't see anyone else. I can take them easily."

"And you figured all of this out, how? By peering through a window? Come on! You're better than that!" Eric retorted, standing up to peer in the window and gain some first-hand incite.
"Yeah...Dude, we need a plan."

Derrick let out another angered huff but didn't try to push past him again.

"What do you see that I don't?"

"Do you see that panel over there? That is the tell-tale sign of the most sophisticated lock-down alarm system in the world. If it is triggered, the entire building becomes completely inaccessible in seconds. No one gets in or out until a revolving override code is initiated both inside the lockdown and from another remote location, simultaneously."

"Oh."

Eric watched his brother's jaw tighten as he sank deep into thought.

"Fine." Derrick finally grumbled. "But we need to be quick."

"No. We need to be smart." Eric insisted.

"That's funny, coming from you." He hissed humorlessly, this time successfully passing Eric. After taking a few steps back towards the fence, Derrick turned around and hissed. "We'd better get a move on. I want to be back here in under two hours."

Eric didn't have a great feeling about the time constraint, but he took solace in the fact that he was giving them that long and decided not to badger him any further.

Chapter 22

On the way back from the diner, having a chance to settle his emotions, after seeing his daughter alive and well, Derrick was thankful that Eric had forced him to work out a plan.

Once he listened to Eric explain his theoretical solution to the lock-down system in a detail that was slightly more showy than informational, he figured it was worth a shot.

It wasn't fool-proof, but it was workable. It made sense, and if nothing else, the plan was a solid, intelligent attempt to complete their mission; as opposed to his blind rage.

Getting back to the house was simple enough.

Except, from the moment the two of them climbed over the gate, they realized that the light was no longer on inside the room.

While that meant that visibility would be more challenging than they hoped, it wasn't a fatal blow to their plan.

Yet, any variation worried Derrick.

Before they even made it back up to the house, he was starting to second-guess the decision he was so confident of not more than ten minutes before.

"Do you think they went to bed?" Eric wondered aloud. "That might make our lives even easier."

"Nothing about this is easy." Derrick retorted but instantly felt bad about snapping at him. "Although, obviously the less feathers we ruffle in the pursuit of getting Eva out of here safely the better."

Eric agreed with a shake of the head before creeping up to the window to get a vantage point.

Derrick watched him intently as a nervous knot formed in the pit of his stomach.

"Oh shit," Eric muttered, turning back to Derrick, his eyes wide.

"What?" Derrick demanded, running up to the window and peering in himself.

The lights were out, but from what he could make out, there seemed to be two bodies sprawled out on the floor.

Fearing that Eva might also be lying among the dead, Derrick ran towards the entrance of the house, no longer caring if he was seen.

He heard Eric try to call after him, but he ignored him. When he reached the front door, he found that it was wide open.

With his heart pounding and his thoughts mocking him, Derrick wasted no time racing into the house. He turned on the light, only to confirm that the man and the woman who he had seen earlier were now casualties of Krone's demented war.

"Don't they work for Krone?" Eric asked as he sidestepped the blood that trailed from the body, originating from a shot to the head.

Again, Derrick didn't care about answering him. Instead, he scoured the rooms, frantically tearing everything he could find apart in pursuit of his daughter.

"Eva?" He called, his voice shaking. "Eva, are you here?"

However, no matter how hard he looked, he found no sign that she had even been here, much less was still here; in any form.

When his fruitless rampage made it back to the living room, where the bodies had fallen, Derrick looked desperately at Eric.

"She was here...Right here."

"I know," Eric replied, but seemed to be thinking. "But, I think the fact that they're here...like this and she isn't, is a good sign." Glancing up, he quickly elaborated. "Well, I mean, first and foremost, she's still alive, but if he had to kill people who work for him, it was likely that he didn't want them to talk if we found them."

"Why would he give a shit? It's not like we'd know what they were talking about anyway. Maybe he killed them because he likes to kill things." Derrick spat.

"No. You're right...About both, but more importantly, about us not having any idea where he would be if he left the property."

For the first time since discovering the bodies, Derrick actually stopped to listen to what Eric was saying.

"Yeah…Okay. So?"

"So, that would stand to reason that they did know how to get to where he took Eva. Or at the very least, we could figure it out." Eric fell back into thought for another moment before his eyes shined with the enlightenment of an epiphany. "I think she's still on the property."

"The cellar," Derrick suggested, almost as a reflex. After he said it, though he consciously pieced together the likelihood of his conclusion. "Yes…The cellar. The one where he shot the video. It must be underneath his house."

With that, Derrick took off, leaving Eric to trail behind once again.

Not wanting to waste a moment, Derrick ran desperately around the house until he found the enterance to the cellar that was lavishly designed to match the rest of the house.

Eric caught up with him as he opened the doors.

Derrick caught Eric's gaze, silently demanding to know what his next move would be if he went down there. Would Eric follow or did he have another plan?

"Let's go," Eric answered in an assuring voice.

Derrick grabbed his gun, cocked the hammer and held it close to him as he descended the stairs.

Eric was close behind.

At the end of the stairs, Derrick saw the same dirt floor that he had in the video and when he looked around the large room, he had no doubt that this was where it was filmed.

In person, the room was even creepier than it was on the video. The whitewashed walls were filthy and smeared with what could be anything from blood and bile to dirt and debris. The floor was gritty and the ceiling was covered with the cobwebs that clung to the rafters. The dank, corroding stench of mold and neglect caused the atmosphere to seem uncharacteristically dense.

"Daddy!" Eva called from the other side of the cellar almost immediately after he had walked down the stairs. Through that one word, Derrick could decipher both intense relief and foreboding fear.

Derrick turned hastily and ran towards the voice.

As he got closer, he realized that she was trapped in a cage that resembled a jail cell.

"Eva!" He exclaimed, grasping the hand she had shoved through the bars, reaching towards him. "I love you. We're gonna go home."

Knowing that she was so close and yet, still in so much danger was a strange feeling. Now that he had found her, all he wanted to do was free her.

However, he knew almost immediately, he wouldn't get that option without having to fight for it.

"Daddy!" Eva screamed, immediately cowering and breaking their connection so that she could shield her eyes.

Derrick turned at exactly the right time to see a man charging at him with a knife.

Unable to use the gun at such a short range, Derrick dropped it and grabbed the man's arm, wrenching it around. The man screamed as Derrick flung him against the bars. Holding him there, he tried to decide his next move.

However, before he did anything seriously violent, he rose his head up and connected with Eva's fearful gaze.

"It's okay, Eva. We're gonna go home, but for now, close your eyes and keep your head down until I say it's alright." Derrick insisted and Eva did as she was told, crouching down and burying her head in her knees.

Once Derrick was sure Eva wasn't looking, he violently slammed the guy's head into the bars, knocking him out and instantly initiating Derrick's fighter instincts. With a quick pivot, he dodged another attack by an incoming henchman.

Derrick threw the unconscious man at the second attacker before shoving himself into the mix of bodies.

Across the room, Derrick caught a glimpse of Eric fighting another clot of Krone's men.

Soon enough, another wave came after him. Two of the men had a knife, while the third man pointed a gun at him.

Derrick's first thought was to get the man with the gun away from Eva and so, he hastily changed his direction before starting the fight.

The man slung the gun out to shoot, but Derrick leaped after the man's hand, grabbed his wrist and yanked him forward. The gun went off near Derrick's feet, but he knew it wouldn't hit him. Instead of worrying about the bullet, he drew his knee up and using the force of the man's momentum he felt the man's ribs shatter as he bucked upward. Derrick followed up his attack with a front-kick to his broken ribs, propelling the man backward.

Derrick grabbed the gun out of the man's hand as fell.

After quickly glancing back at Eva to ensure she wasn't watching, he pulled the trigger twice, shooting on of each of the assailants' hands. As their knives clattered to the floor, Derrick struck them both in the head with the butt of his gun before kicking the knives away.

When Derrick looked up, he saw that Krone was fighting Eric. There didn't seem to be any other bodyguards around.

Finally!

Derrick thought as he took a few steps towards Krone with every intention of giving him what he deserved.

However, before he could reach them, he watched as Krone produced a dagger, lunging it threateningly against Eric.

Eric's gun was lying on the ground and while Derrick momentarily thought about using his gun on his father, he instantly decided that would be far too merciful for him.

Eric masterfully dodged the stabs of the dagger, until one misstep allowed Krone to turn a block into an offensive attack. He shoved Eric backward.

Before Eric could recover, Krone rushed forward, with the dagger in position to strike. Eric tried to block the blow, but the force of the thrust caught him off guard.

Almost as though in slow motion, Krone thrust the dagger, evading Eric's defense with brute force and plunged the blade deep into Eric's chest.

Eric stopped, gasping for breath as he gaped down at the blade buried up to its sheath as the blood started to stain his shirt.

Derrick stopped dead; his breath catching abruptly in the back of his throat.

As Eric fell to his knees, he looked up at Krone with defiant hate in his eyes as his body started to shimmer with a blue haze.

He sneered at Krone as the discoloration became more illuminated.

Soon after, Eric disappeared, leaving only the dagger as it clattered to the ground and a sprinkling of ash behind.

Chapter 23

No matter how many times Derrick watched his family members die, it never got any easier.

Yet, as the pain he felt culminated in his mind, he forced himself to channel it directly towards Krone.

Letting go of all his inhibitions, he charged at him.

Krone hardly had time to turn around before his face collided with Derrick's fist.

Krone staggered back, blood spewing out of his mouth and a rattle of pain echoing from his throat.

Instantly, Derrick followed him. Grabbing Krone by the lapels of his azure suit jacket he yanked him forward, turned him around and slammed him back against a wall. Without wasting any time, he punched Krone repeatedly. The first two blows landed on either side of his head, while the third connected with his solar plexus, causing Krone to keel over. Instinctively, Derrick planted both hands behind Krone's head and drove his knee up, while forcing Krone's face down, striking him perfectly, staggering him.

Still dazed, Krone turned around and swung at Derrick, but he blocked it, grabbed his arm and threw it around to the back of him. Wrenching it up, he shoved Krone back into the wall, smashing his face against it.

"Derrick, be reasonable..." Krone huffed after a failed attempt to overpower his son. "You don't want to kill me in front of your daughter, do you? What kind of example would that set?"

"Oh, I'm not just going to kill you." Derrick hissed back, shoving Krone up against the wall with a force that almost splintered his spine.

Derrick heard the sound of cartilage crunching and flesh grinding against bone as Krone connected with the wall and it brought Derrick a glimmer of vengeful satisfaction.

His attempt to appeal to Derrick's humanity fell on deaf ears. His overriding rage and the degree of disdain he held for his father should've bothered him.

But it didn't.

"What was it you told Eric?" Derrick growled. "That he was going to wish he could die on a daily basis? I will personally ensure that you know exactly what that threat entails."

With that, Derrick threw Krone to the ground and prepared to stomp that smug, thin face until it shattered.

However, before he could, Krone rolled back and reared himself up defensively, holding a syringe in his hand.

Derrick dodged the stab, which missed him by mere inches before he turned and grabbed the wrist that held the syringe.

The dirty fighting tactic only enraged Derrick further. Within a crazed bout of ire, Derrick twisted Krone's hand until he heard it snap and the syringe fell from it. Derrick kicked Krone backward and reached down to grab the needle.

Krone recovered and attacked Derrick, shoving him onto the ground.

Krone hit him in the face as he held him down, his forearm, now with another dagger in it, pressed on Derrick's throat.

Ignoring the blade, he pushed back and twisted away from the attack as Krone tried to slide the weapon across his throat.

With the split second he gained, he leaped up and, grabbing Krone, he slammed him against the ground.

Krone blindly jabbed the blade as they wrestled, slitting opened Derrick's arm

However, with the amount of adrenaline pumping through his veins, Derrick never felt it.

He was fighting for not only his survival but, more importantly, the survival of his daughter.

Derrick knew that if he so much as hesitated, Eva was as good as dead, or worse.

Therefore, instead of allowing the pierce of the blade or the flow of the blood to distract him, he raised the syringe high in the air and struck it down, putting the sum of his pain and fury into the blow.

Krone tried to protect himself from the force of the attack, but Derrick wouldn't allow him another chance to hurt his family again.

He felt the needle pierce through soft tissue of Krone's left eye easily, only being stopped by the base of the filled syringe.

Shock reverberated through Krone as Derrick imagined his vision dimming, with the last image it saw being the threat of the needle.

Krone screamed out in pain as Derrick injected the contents of the syringe into his eye without remorse, causing him to immediately go limp.

Realizing that Krone was incapacitated, Derrick pushed away from him, eager to get Eva to safety.

Once he did, he was sure he would be able to return and finish enacting his revenge.

Without wasting another second, Derrick searched Krone's pockets for a key, determining that since he was in a hurry, it was probably still on his person. After a moment, in the inside, breast pocket, Derrick found what he was after.

Hastily, he rushed back over to the cell where Eva was still hiding, curled up in a ball.

"Everything's okay, Eva." He called, taking stock of the carnage that surrounded them. "But don't look up. You don't need to see this..."

He picked up the lock that was used to secure the door and prayed the key would work.

Thankfully, it fit perfectly into the padlock and opened it promptly.

The second Eva heard the door squeak opened, she jumped up and ran into Derrick's arms.

"Daddy!" She exclaimed, fresh tears immediately tumbling down her face. "I knew you'd find me." She whispered as Derrick held her close and did his best to shield her from the terror that surrounded her.

"Always." He assured, kissing her hair, before turning around and making a mad dash for the top of the cellar stairs.

As he climbed out of the cellar, a figure appeared before him and he readied himself for a fight.

"I come in peace!" Eric exclaimed, raising his hands in surrender. "Dying once in a day is plenty for me, thanks!"

Seeing him, Derrick sighed with relief as Eva poked her head up.

"Uncle Eric?" She called, beaming brightly at him.

"Hey, Eva!" His eyes looked relieved as he breathed out a long sigh. "Thank God." He huffed, almost completely under his breath. "I was afraid..." He stopped short. "Never mind."

"So, where did you ghost to?" Derrick asked, arching an eyebrow.

"I wanted more pie..." He grinned.

"Ghost? Pie? What are you guys talking about?" Eva's eyes passed between her father and her uncle suspiciously as she spoke. "How'd you get out here?"

"It's a long story, for another day," Eric beamed at her.

At first, Eva seemed as though she was going to insist, but eventually, she drew in a deep, exhausted breath as she sagged against Derrick.

"I'm okay with that..." She replied, letting out a yawn.

"Thanks." Eric teased before looking past Derrick into the darkness of the stairwell. "So, I guess you're good?"

"Almost." As Derrick spoke, a sly grin crossed his features. "Can you take Eva back to the truck? There's something I need to take care of."

When Eric's gaze caught Derrick's his head shook knowingly.

"Absolutely."

Derrick nodded a thank you, handed Eva to Eric and walked back down the stairs, to finish this once and for all.

Despite the fact that Eva was safe, Derrick was still haunted by the terror that he had brought upon his family. With every step back towards the man who had reduced his life to cinders, his anger contorted his mind. His fury and pain bubbled to the surface. Hate engulfed him and thoughts of the vendetta he was going to take out against his father provided him with a strange sense of solace.

He wasn't particularly proud of himself, but he knew what needed to be done. He wanted to hurt Krone like he had hurt his family.

He wanted to show him the same sadistic mercy that he showed Lily when he slit her throat and the same cruel commiseration he portrayed when he told Eva that her parents no longer wanted her.

Derrick wanted to bleed, bruise, and singe Krone with his sins. Killing him would come, eventually, but that was only so that he couldn't come after Eva again. It wasn't because he thought the old man deserved a sliver of forbearance.

If he could, he would spend an eternity making Krone pay for what he did to his family and that still wouldn't be enough.

Yet, he realized that thankfully, he still had a life to live. He might have lost Lily, but he still had Eva and she was everything to him.

First, however, Derrick had to ensure that this bastard was good and dead.

When Derrick reached the bottom of the stairs, there was an eerie sense of solidarity that washed over him. He realized that Krone was likely still knocked out, but the sensation of being alone was overwhelming.

That's impossible... Derrick thought as he turned the corner and pulled his gun, ready for a one-eyed attack, in case he was mistaken.

Carefully, Derrick inched back to the corner where he had left Krone. It took a moment for his eyes to adjust to the dim lighting, but as he grew closer, he couldn't believe what his eyes were showing him.

Frantically, he checked the entirety of the cellar, but to his utter shock and surprise, it was completely empty.

Krone was nowhere to be found.

Feeling a burning sense of rage prickle up his spine, he ran back over to where he knew he had left Krone's unconscious body.

He peered into the dirt and something caught his eye.

That was when he was sure that Krone was gone.

All that remained was a small pool of blood...and a flash drive.

www.ingramcontent.com/pod-product-compliance
Lightning Source LLC
Chambersburg PA
CBHW031305170626
46807CB00001B/317